2030

2030

NOTHING IS WHAT IT SEEMS

J.P. Ozuna

CONTENTS

ACKNOWLEDGMENTS

Writing a book is far more challenging than I expected and more gratifying than I could imagine. I am beyond grateful to my editor, family, and friends. Especially:

Rosalin Ozuna, my fantastic sister, for your invaluable help in caring for my young toddlers as I worked tirelessly to bring this story to life. No tengo palabras qué puedan expresar mi agradecimiento.

My partner Derek Bruno you are our rock.

Angeline Ozuna, my beloved sister, for your encouragement and support so happy I can journey through life with you.

My cousins Leodith Valdez, Michelle Hernandez, John Bourdierd, Melissa Bobadilla, and Maria Regalado.

Author Benjamin Burgess for inspiring me to follow my dream and guiding me through it. I appreciate all your support.

Johanna Lamarche, you believed in me from day one; you read my story as I wrote it and loved it. Had it not been for you, I'm not sure I would have seen this through. Thank you for embarking on this literary and publishing journey with me, there is no way I could've done any of this without you, and I am forever grateful.

I appreciate you, my loyal friends who have encouraged and supported me. Especially Vernice Infante, Geraldo De La Cruz, and Alexandra Aracena.

To my beloved readers, you are why I write. Thank you for letting me entertain you. I hope this story can impact you in meaningful ways.

Lastly, to my magnificent children Nathaniel Lopez, Jade Bruno, and Anisha Bruno, you inspire me to be the best version of myself, and everything I do is for you. I love you unconditionally.

PART ONE

The gunshots were deafening, but she kept running as fast as possible. Her lungs burned and ached. She felt warm blood flowing down her back as her black T-shirt under a black leather jacket clung to her skin.

Everything seemed blurred, and they continued hunting her down like an animal, shooting with utter disregard for the passersby.

Mothers pushing strollers, children playing, construction work taking place, the joggers, and those enjoying a beverage at a sidewalk café were of no significance. The only thing that mattered was her execution.

The bustling city felt like the concrete jungle it is known for as she attempted to escape from her pursuers. People ducked and moved out of the way but were otherwise unfazed as if this was no unusual occurrence … or like they were numb.

She sprinted in and out of traffic, getting good traction from her black combat boots as she ran and used vehicles and buildings as cover, shooting and killing a few of the ones following her, but their pursuit was relentless. She wasn't sure how many they had sent after her, but it seemed like an army.

Orion, her employer, has unlimited influence and resources at their disposal. It would only be a matter of time before they captured her, but she knew she had to survive another day. The information she had stolen from the corporation was too important, and she had to get it to the only person she could trust.

She was losing a great deal of blood, and now her weapon was out of ammunition. There was a train station nearby, so she rushed to it, hoping to get away before losing consciousness. Her attempt was successful; she ran into the station, leaving a bloody trail.

The turnstile seemed like a six-foot solid wall. As Onyx excruciatingly got over it, there was already a train there, and she flung herself in before the doors closed. Then, as the train sped away, she felt everything going dark.

She could taste blood in her mouth, and her breathing was agonizing. "NO" she screamed, knowing she would be in the hospital and their custody if she passed out.

The passengers looked at her, horrified. Even the blue jeans she was wearing were stained red. They ripped on the inner thigh as she jumped across the turnstile.

She was amused at how pathetic the other passengers looked in their stupid masks, convinced by using them that they were safe from viruses. Perhaps they looked appalled, not because she was bleeding to death, but because she wasn't wearing a mask herself.

They weren't required to wear them any longer, but that's the thing with people. Once you condition them, there's no turning back. Even if you show them irrefutable proof that the mask won't work, they will continue wearing them as a safety net. So, it's no longer a physical act but psychological manipulation.

"Oh, I'm sorry. I forgot to grab my fucking mask before getting shot and jumping on the train," she yelled, laughing hysterically and attempting to get onto her feet. A Good Samaritan tried to help her, but she growled at him like a wounded animal.

Using an empty seat, she raised herself onto it and sat, attempting to catch her breath. People stared and began to move away as if she were a leper. She laughed out loud and grunted in pain.

A few stops later, she got off the train. Of course, it would've been foolish to do so at the following stop because that's what they expected her to do, but staying on that train too long was suicide.

They'd have all local law enforcement swarming the stations swiftly, and her fellow passengers would surely snitch to inform authorities that there was a bleeding, maskless psycho on board.

The thought made her smile as she hurriedly climbed the stairs at the nearest exit. Some of those stations were a maze. Finally, outside, she quickly scanned the area. There was an abandoned building across the street, and hastily, she made her way to it.

As soon as she was safely inside, she assessed all her injuries, lowering the backpack she was carrying front side to protect her vital organs. She laughed because she should've had a second one for her back, or perhaps a ballistic vest would've been more suitable, but there was no time to prepare.

She was lucky enough to retrieve the bag in the first place. The bag's contents were mainly medical supplies, antibiotics, and morphine. Of course, she had some metal plates protecting the laptop.

She examined it to see if it was damaged during her escape and found it intact. Time was of the essence; she began tending her gunshot wounds rapidly, knowing that all hands were on deck searching for her.

She discovered a floor panel that appeared to move as she went through the building. Lifting it, she found a stash of money, not that she needed any. Using cash was frowned upon these days. However, the revolver in there was what she was most excited about. It looked old, but it had three rounds that could come in handy.

She had some ammunition in the bag for her 9mm pistol but trying to find it would've meant a certain death when she used whatever magazines she was carrying on her belt.

New York City had fallen into crime, and many residents had fled to other states. Florida was now a sovereign nation. You needed a visa to enter. Texas was working toward independence, and everything had gone to shit in less than a decade.

After the pandemic and ensuing monkey sham, renters who were behind on rent were not allowed to get evicted. As a result, many landlords filed for bankruptcy and left that state, leaving the residents to fend for themselves. Many had no heat, and many houses and buildings were uninhabited. Now, the city was a dreadful scene.

Only certain areas still looked attractive and were heavily patrolled and strictly reserved for the "elite." You know, those pretending to work hard to make things "inclusive and fair for all."

Surveillance drones patrolled the skies to combat crime and monitor residents, and anyone speaking against the government was an enemy of the state and held prisoner for conspiracy. Likewise, anyone questioning the CDC got locked away for spreading hostile misinformation.

Most people now lived in government-owned green zone set-tlements where they received food, clothes, and anything else they needed, but there was a curfew and restricted access to the internet. Most people were unemployed and spent their time in the Metaverse.

The wealthy carried on as though nothing ever happened. Working for security contractors was the closest thing to normalcy for the aver-age Joe like her. If you work for one of those corporations, there are some liberties, and you can afford to pay rent and live life without certain restrictions.

Retracing her steps, Onyx cleaned away all traces of blood. The hideaway under the floor was small, but she would try to squeeze into it in the fetal position. Her ass and legs were too big for this space, but she needed to rest to regain her strength. She will need it.

Kyle arrived just as the train was departing. He knew she had gotten on because the trail of blood had ended at the platform's edge. He wore an ugly maroon polo and khaki cargo pants with tactical boots.

She was too savvy. She could outsmart the best of them. *What if she didn't get on the train?* he thought, agitated, sweating, and sec-ond-guessing himself.

"Fuck" he screamed. "Set a perimeter. Search this entire station. I want men searching the tunnels in both directions, checking every exit and hole. I want that bitch found *yesterday*!" he screamed.

His thoughts were scattered. So many possibilities. He had to get this right. He raced back out of the station. Onyx would probably get off at the next stop while everyone was wasting time here.

Running to his car, he pulled out his phone. "I want a team with me at the next station. I'm going to find this whore and blow her brains out," he said.

The car door had barely shut, and the car was on the drive. His urgency was palpable. This situation was catastrophic. Everything he had worked for was now in jeopardy.

He was going a hundred miles per hour on a city street. Unhinged and furious, every muscle in his body was tense, and he could feel the hatred like a vile poison coursing through his veins.

There was nothing he wanted more than to tear her brains out through her neck. He'd like to dismember her. He wished he could stomp her eyeballs after ripping them from her skull. He wanted blood. But instead, he gripped the steering wheel so tightly that his knuckles turned white.

He sped in and out of traffic lanes screaming and shouting, recklessly endangering those around him.

Orion's facial recognition software attempted to locate her, utilizing every drone and city camera available and operational.

Suddenly, the car screeched to a halt. Another vehicle had stopped, and three other Orion agents stepped out.

"Cover the exits!" Kyle instructed, "Make sure she doesn't get away, and if you find her, I want her alive. I'll kill the bitch myself," he barked.

He ran into the station, looked around, and didn't see many people, so he carefully studied the floor for signs of blood and saw nothing out of order.

"Motherfucker, where are you?" he bellowed.

He would have to review the footage for all stations in the area, which would waste time. In addition, Onyx would have a big lead, making finding her even more difficult.

Defeated, he sent out mass texts asking for updates. All were negative, and he was livid. In addition, Kyle's clothes were wet with sweat, and his shirt stuck to his skin like glue, further aggravating him.

He returned to Orion Security headquarters in downtown Manhattan to brief the boss, Simon.

Kyle took the ramp to the underground parking lot, speeding, and swiped the side of his truck with the wall.

"Motherfucker! Fuck you, bitch," he cursed.

He parked the car, still angry, and placed his hand on the security access pad to the elevator.

"We lost her," he said to Simon.

"When you want something done right, you must do it yourself. All of you are fucking useless," Simon shouted in a rage, veins protruding from his neck and forehead.

He wore a black suit with a navy shirt, no tie, and unbuttoned to the extent you could see his hairy chest.

"Fucking find her. I want that bitch's head on my desk before the end of the day, or I will kill you, Kyle. Do you understand, you piece of shit?" Simon yelled, pounding a fist on the desk.

Kyle nodded. He despised being spoken to like a child and hated this cunt even more. He was going to find Onyx and gut her like a pig.

"Do you think I give a shit about the information she took? Onyx Pion could've stolen the goddamn Holy Grail. No one gives a fuck, Kyle!" he continued as he sat.

"We can lie and deceive, and people won't care. We will pay the media not to cover it or spin some bullshit. What I have a problem with is that bitch tarnishing my fucking reputation. She is a worthless parasitic little cunt, and I want you to find her so that I can make an example of her to anyone getting any ideas. I want her dead!" Simon screamed.

Kyle walked out and lit a cigarette. He felt the blood thickening in his veins, and the anger left a bitter taste in his mouth. He retrieved his phone from his pocket and dialed a number.

"Listen to me very carefully … I want every asset activated. We have a level-one priority, and I need it resolved by midnight. After that, I will text you the information for dissemination," Kyle said.

He took a long pull from his cigarette. "One last thing. If they fail, terminate all of them," he concluded ominously.

He ended the call before the party on the other end could reply. Then Kyle got into his car and drove off. He drove angry and reckless as usual. Simon was a callous man whose cruelty borders that of a sociopath, but Kyle was more afraid of himself. He knew if it came down to it, he would kill Simon.

A man that cannot control his rage will succumb to it, but a man who can control his emotions is unpredictable and dangerous. Simon was a calculating man. There was a reason he had achieved so much. Kyle, on the other hand, was volatile. He coveted Simon's position and would do whatever it took to reach it.

Simon knew this, but for now, Kyle was an excellent bloodhound. Kyle had convinced himself that his ascension to the throne was inevitable; nevertheless, he must accurately strategize every move. An all-out war with Simon would result in inevitable defeat, and all his hard work would have been for nothing.

Patience was the mother of all virtues. When correctly applied, it bears good fruit. He had a plan, but Onyx Pion was now a thorn in his side, and he must terminate her.

Onyx woke up frightened, striking her head with the floor panel. "Shit, one more fucking bruise!" she said, kicking the floorboard out and realizing it was dawn.

She quickly got out, mentally planning every move she would make. Kyle was hunting her. Indeed, he had not stopped, slept, or eaten. He was an obsessive, psychotic maniac and would not rest until he recovered what she had taken.

It was only a matter of time before he caught up with her, and she relished the thought of shredding his head to pieces, but she had to stay focused on her mission.

Onyx redressed her wounds and changed into clean clothes, a fresh navy T-shirt and black jeans from her bag. She wiped the blood from her boots and jacket.

She wore a baseball cap and black sunglasses. The cameras on every street corner wouldn't help, and neither would the drones.

Certainly, Kyle would access them in his desperation to track her movements. She decided to exit the building through the back alleyway. There wouldn't be any cameras back there.

Although surveillance drones flying around would likely ensure her capture, there was no escaping this Orwellian nightmare.

She had to stay ten steps ahead. Kyle's anger blinded him, making him sloppy, irrational, and predictable.

No one on the face of the earth hated her more than him, yet that was to her advantage because anger blinds reason, and he was one angry motherfucker.

She wasn't angry. She was determined; nothing was more important than tearing the organization down. She decided to walk to her destination, which would benefit her from not being caught off guard or ambushed.

She stopped at a food cart on the corner and used the cart's umbrella to conceal herself. The vendor served his customers quickly. It wasn't that cold, but he was wearing a winter hat which Onyx found amusing. She ordered a muffin with black coffee and kept moving.

It would be more difficult to track her if she's on the move. She was already a few hours behind. This concrete jungle was precisely that: a jungle. How she despised it. Overcrowded, dirty, and loud, the noise was what she loathed the most.

Building demolitions brought giant cranes with noisy machinery everywhere, drilling holes into the sidewalks and streets, all for more green zones—a hideous disaster.

Onyx grew up in foster care. Both her parents died before she was five years old. They immigrated from the Dominican Republic while her mother was pregnant with her, and she had no recollection of them.

She liked to fantasize about what life with them could have been when she was younger. Onyx spent hours escaping reality in a fake world she had created in her imagination, where her parents were loving and caring. She imagined she had a sister, and they went on exciting adventures. That helped her cope, and she found reading a sweet escape from real life. Although some of her foster parents were decent people, most of them only did it for the money.

She never went hungry or lacked a place to sleep but never connected with anyone. It was a foreign concept to her how people could walk around hand in hand. It made her uncomfortable to see people embrace each other. None of her foster parents ever hugged or kissed her, so she'd never been comfortable with human affections.

Alma was the closest thing she had as a family. The last foster home she lived in was while she was fifteen to eighteen before she joined the Marine Corps.

Alma was the pastor's wife, who had a church downstairs from the building she lived in Washington Heights.

Onyx remembered the gentrification protest happening in her neighborhood. It seemed insignificant at the time. However, now, she realized the plan was to displace low-income families and small businesses so the area could eventually end up in green zones.

Climate change was huge back then too. That was the catalyst. People would not have volunteered to crowd themselves into shoe boxes otherwise—a genius move.

Every Friday, when Onyx came home from school, she would see

Alma sweeping the sidewalk in front of the church. She always greeted her with a warm, genuine smile. Onyx knew it was sincere.

She had developed an incredibly acute ability to read people and concluded that most people were phony, putting up a façade, desperately seeking approval, and pretending to be happy.

Not Alma. She was happy, she was kind, and she was honest. However, those three years were rough. The foster lady she lived with was a drunk. She never had food for the smaller kids and was entirely unfit for the role.

Onyx only wanted to get through those years so she could get out of that godforsaken house and city. But unfortunately, she felt sorry for the two younger kids that lived there.

No child should go hungry, so she often snuck food from the fast-food restaurant she worked at, part time, after school, to bring home for the kids.

Onyx was introverted back then. She had no friends and didn't care to make any. So she spoke to no one but Alma and her school counselor occasionally.

Alma seemed to be aware of everything. Onyx was returning home from her shift on a Friday night, and the church service ended when Alma called her over.

"Young lady, can you help me with these trash bags?" Alma asked.

Onyx looked around to ensure she was speaking to her. Then she silently grabbed a trash bag resting against the church door, seeing no one else there.

"Thank you," the petite lady said as they walked to the side of the building where the trash dumpsters were. Alma had long, brown hair she always kept in a braid and wore a long dress down to her ankles. She had a gentle, almost melodic voice and caring brown eyes with radiant tanned skin. Onyx found her to be one of the prettiest ladies. Perhaps her beautiful soul emanated from within, making her even more attractive.

"We had a lot of food for this evening's youth service. So you're welcome to bring it home," Alma said to Onyx.

Onyx didn't like seeming like a charity case, but she swallowed her pride and nodded. The kids were always hungry, and she couldn't bring food for them that night.

From that day on, Alma found small ways to reach Onyx, and despite her hesitation, Onyx allowed Alma into her life. The rare moments of vulnerability that she ever experienced were with her.

Now, she was running for her life, and there was no time for weakness. Kyle would have his very best searching for her, and there were only two people in the world she trusted, Alma being one of them.

The other was Mateo, the only other friend she had and the one who helped her join the military.

Orion was employed internationally, and many government contracts involved the Central Intelligence Agency. Though Orion was a private company, it modeled its training on the CIA. The best assets were overseas, but most could quickly return stateside within a few hours.

Kyle felt uneasy. This traitor is one of their best assets, an agent with high cognitive capabilities and absolute emotional restraint, and she was strictly rational. He always envied Onyx because he was explosive and irrational.

During their Orion training, he could never beat her out of the top spot, and he detested coming second to Onyx Pion.

Her disconnect from her feelings allowed her to evaluate everything logically. It set her apart and gave her a broader awareness.

On the other hand, rage is blinding and often conceals important minor details that can be the difference between life and death.

Most assets responded well to the mRNA enhancements and empathetic suppression treatments. Still, the side effects in many, if not all, were extreme rage, which could be problematic when applied to the average person. However, Onyx Pion was everything *but* average.

Orion spent a lot of resources and time training its security personnel. Many of them had served in the armed forces. Onyx excelled above all. She was good at combat training, weapons, psychological operations, and physical endurance, and her ability to adapt to physiological enhancements positively was unparalleled.

Kyle pulled over and bashed the steering wheel, imagining it was her head. "FUCK FUCK FUCK fuck, you bitch!" he growled.

His vision was distorting the whole scenery. He could see dots floating around in front of him. Everything appeared more diminutive, and there was no color, only shades of gray with hints of red in his peripheral. He closed his eyes and took deep breaths. The stupid doctor he saw monthly told him he should do that when he fits into a rage while she injected him with a vitamin cocktail and a conniving smile on her face.

He took deep, slow breaths, calming himself. Finding Onyx as soon as possible was his primary objective because he had more important matters to resolve, and this was taking up too much of his precious time. And in his case, time wasn't just money—it was a whole damn empire.

This matter was too important to leave in the hands of space cadets. So, Kyle was going to take matters into his own hands. He would ensure they get Onyx because no one is better than him. He will prove that he is number one—once and for all.

PART TWO

Finally, Onyx managed to reach her destination undetected, perceivably. She only hoped that she was not endangering anyone.

Only a few buildings remained, and the church, *by the grace of God*, Onyx thought. The rest of the neighborhood was a green zone with tall walls surrounding the complex, topped with barbed wire and excessive cameras.

As Onyx moved closer to the church, she looked around, not because she thought someone was following her, but because she did not want to be recognized. She had not left any friends behind when she enlisted, but it would be best if she did not attract unnecessary attention.

Although only about three buildings were still standing, and everyone else was tucked away in a green-zone shoe box, she doubted if that could be a problem.

Onyx wasn't worried that Kyle would track her here unless he spotted her on surveillance, which she knew would take time. Even the best facial recognition software would have difficulty identifying her with the hat, sunglasses, and mask.

The address she used for her military application was her high school. Turning eighteen in April allowed her to apply without parental consent and leave immediately after graduation. Luckily, she disregarded Mateo when he suggested she use his address while enlisting. He was her recruiter.

Onyx deliberately planned everything. She had meticulously prearranged how she would free herself since she was twelve. Moreover, the high school she attended was a specialized one in the Bronx, so if Kyle were going to dig into her past, he would have a hard time tracking her down.

The church gate was up. *Alma is likely setting up for the Friday youth service*, Onyx thought, walking past and around the side to the dumpsters.

She saw an emergency exit and a small window leading to the church basement. She pried it open and crawled into a small utility room. Opening the door slowly and quietly, she scanned the room to see if anyone was there but only saw Alma placing food over a large table.

She waited a few minutes, ensuring that Alma was alone. Then, feeling confident that no one else was there, she gently entered the room and closed her door.

She didn't want to startle her. Alma was singing, *"open the eyes of my heart, Lord,"* so Onyx walked over to the stairs. She climbed up unnoticed and examined the church. She saw no one there, so she went to the main entrance and locked it.

"Alma," Onyx loudly called out as she walked closer to the basement door.

Alma was still singing praises, *"I want to see you,"* and could not hear her, but as she started down the stairs, Alma turned around and saw her.

"Onyx, is that you?" she asked excitedly, coming closer. "Wow, it *is* you! I thought I would never see you again. I pray for you every day, sweetheart. How are you doing?"

Alma wore her traditional long dress, and her hair was in her usual braid, although now Onyx saw streaks of gray adorning it. Nevertheless, she was still as beautiful as Onyx remembered.

Now, Onyx was starting to feel like this was a bad idea, and she regretted coming here and involving Alma with all this.

"Hey, Alma, you haven't aged a day," Onyx said. An awkward silence permeated the air as Alma stared at her.

Onyx always felt bare when Alma watched her that way, like she was peering into her soul as if she could read everything Onyx was going through.

"Listen, I'm sorry to show up like this, but I had no one to turn to with this situation, and I need a huge favor. Can you help me?" Onyx pleaded.

Alma opened a folding chair and signaled for her to sit. Onyx wanted to hurry through this visit and keep moving, but instead, she sat.

Then Alma walked to the table and poured some tea into a cup from a thermos. "Here you go," she said, handing Onyx the cup.

Onyx drank the tea, and surprisingly, it was comforting and refreshing.

"Alma, I have a flash drive containing vital information, but before I give it to you, I need to give you full disclosure. I obtained it illegally, and there's a dangerous organization after me. They will take extreme measures to get it back. Orion is hunting me down, and if they succeed, they will kill me," Onyx told her.

Alma observed Onyx tapping her knees with her fingers and chewing her inner lip. Her eyes looked wild, and she seemed like a cornered, rabid animal.

She reached over and took Onyx's hands. Onyx tensed at the touch, but Alma held them tightly. She wanted to hug her and tell her that she was there for her and had always been there.

"My child, though I walk through the valley of the shadow of death, I will fear no evil. On the contrary, I will help you with whatever you need," she said, gripping her hands reassuringly.

Onyx took a deep breath. She admired Alma's commitment and her resolve. She knew that Alma would give her life for her God, what she believed in, and what she perceived as righteous. That kind of conviction deserved respect.

Alma agreed to secure the flash drive and keep their meeting confidential. They would not involve anyone else in the matter. Alma wouldn't even mention it to her husband, the pastor, for he would probably give Onyx up, not wanting to conceal the truth, and she would not put him in that predicament.

"Only God and I will know, and he hears our prayers," Alma said.

Onyx left the way she came. She didn't want street cameras to capture her exiting the church, which would endanger Alma and the entire congregation.

There was someone else she had to see. Mateo. He wasn't just her recruiter but a mentor and friend.

Despite only being three years older than her when they first met, he seemed wise beyond his years, and at the time, in her naiveté, he was the most intelligent person she knew. He helped her through the enlisting process and with her physical training. After all, he had a black belt in karate and practiced jujitsu.

Mateo was also the only guy she had ever felt any physical attraction for, possibly because he was the only one she had ever spent time with, and their relationship eventually turned sexual. The word "romantic" would be inappropriate because Onyx was utterly emotionally unavailable.

She always felt that he wanted more from their friendship, but the only thing she wanted was to get away and forget the life she had once lived. She wanted a fresh start.

During her time in the military, she was wholly absorbed with training and did not entertain any suitors. However, she met some wonderful people, many of whom she would die for, and she was confident they would do the same for her, but none she allowed to get too close.

Mateo had warned her to keep to herself and not be disappointed by those only looking to get in her pants, not that she cared. She wasn't on a quest to find love, but she knew it was genuine advice. They had casual sex, but they were friends above all. So she decided to keep it simple. The last thing she wanted was for Mateo to think they would have a relationship when she went off to basic training.

Mateo will not condone what she has done, but he would support her. Of that, she was sure. So, the plan was to give him another copy of the file and stash the original within the laptop she had taken from Pharma Corp, which Orion had assigned her.

Onyx had managed to copy the file from a computer in Pharma Corp onto her laptop. They have strict measures to know when something happens and discovered her transgression sooner than Onyx expected, which caused her violent, hasty escape.

It felt selfish to jeopardize the only people she trusted and cared about, but that's what life is about: giving your life, if necessary, for those you love, the things you believe in, and the moral integrity to do what is right, even when it is not popular.

Humans need connection, support, and something to live for to be happy. That kept her going, and she hoped no harm would come to Mateo or Alma. One thing she knew for sure: she could not do it alone.

Onyx was on high alert, constantly looking over her shoulder, exhausted and paranoid. She longed for all this to be over. But instead, she felt trapped in a nightmare. Although she never had affection and didn't seem to need it, she wanted someone to embrace her and tell her everything would be all right. Those were always fleeting thoughts and emotions. Onyx talked herself out of those fragile states of mind and told herself she was more than capable of overcoming this. She knew she was strong and adept enough to accomplish her goal of bringing Pharma Corp down. One foot in front of the other, one day at a time … "I got this!" she mumbled as she sped up.

The phone buzzed in his pocket, and Kyle fumbled it, dropping it on the ground. Then he picked it up and angrily answered.

"What? It better be good, Steve. I swear if it's not good, I'm going to lose my shit," Kyle warned him, agitated.

"We followed up on a lead to an abandoned building. From some footage we reviewed, we got a facial recognition hit. I sent a team out there but came up with nothing. So I have tech people combing through footage from city cameras. I'll let you know as soon as we get anything else," Steve said.

Kyle inhaled and exhaled loudly. "Steve, I need you to find her. We must end this as soon as possible and have human resources pull her file. I want to know every fucking thing about her. I want a detailed chronological report of her life, from birth to now, ASAP. I want her military records. Our contact at the CIA can help with that. Make sure you explain the severity of the situation and the implications and tell him we could use a hand. Pharma Corp is a big client, and they are furious. They want the files she took and us to mitigate the situation. If we lose our contract with them, it will have severe repercussions globally for the company. Could you send me the location of the building? I'm going to go out there myself," Kyle said.

Kyle went to the abandoned building and silently stood there, attempting to piece together her actions. *You can see her staggering here in the video. She didn't die. There's no dead body, no footage of her exiting. Could she still be in there hiding? If so? Where?*

He felt the anger rising within him. He took a deep breath and meticulously inspected every inch of the place. Finally, he came upon a floorboard that appeared to move and bent down to pull it up. It was a fair-sized space, and Onyx could easily fit in it.

He scrutinized every inch of that space and saw what appeared to be blood. Onyx *had* been there. Where would she go? Was there anyone that could help her? He knew nothing. She was an enigma and never talked about her personal life or hung out.

Kyle was bitter because she rejected him on several occasions. She beat him at everything, but she also refused his sexual advances, which angered him. He told everyone she was into girls to make himself feel better, and since no one knew anything about her, it could very well be true.

There was absolutely nothing to go on. Yet, ironically, those are the best people to recruit in this business. No family. No friends. No life. No one would inquire or complain if they went MIA.

They work long hours, seven days a week, on holidays, with no complaints. This is their life, but no one expects to be hunting one of their own because those qualities that make them the perfect candidates also make it impossible to track them.

People seek comfort when they are running or hiding. They tend to go back to what is familiar. They seek help, but usually from people they can trust, and as far as he knew, Onyx had no one. He thought she preferred it that way, but if she wasn't going to seek help, how would she do it?

The obvious on-the-run rules are to keep a low profile and don't remain in the same place too long. But Onyx was unusual. She had a different thought process.

They went through Orion training together. He knew her somewhat and was glad she lacked ambition because if she wanted, she would have been running things for Simon—not him.

Simon saw Onyx as his prize recruit. He didn't only want her to run all his operations but wanted her as his mate. So when she refused him, he gave her a mediocre post with Pharma Corp.

Kyle knew for sure that she had the advantage. She got away initially, and if they had not found her yet, they were likely not going to.

Running from Pharma Corp is ludicrous, absolute insanity. Now she understood what David felt facing Goliath and hoped she was as successful as he was.

However, she was committed to seeing this through, even if it killed her. Things were complex. Onyx didn't work directly for Pharma Corp, but Orion Security, which employs personnel with military experience and top security clearance since they also have black ops government contracts.

High-profile corporations utilize Orion personnel for their security. In addition, Orion has worldwide prestige because of its contract with governments. So these companies figure that if they are good enough for the government, they are good enough for us, and they assume correctly. Still, if Orion doesn't contain the Onyx situation soon, it could spell disaster for billions of dollars.

Taking on Pharma Corp also involved taking on Orion. Although it seemed impossible, once she destroyed Pharma Corp, she was coming for Orion and its top employers. But for now, one battle at a time.

What she had uncovered at Pharma Corp was dangerous because it interconnected all the agencies. They're all in concert, which made this particularly difficult. Onyx did not have a plan. She acted on impulse, which was uncharacteristic, but she saw an opportunity—and seized it.

Her assignment to a high-profile scientist's security detail, who also had a contract with the Centers for Diseases Control, afforded her access to confidential and sensitive information.

Often the most extraordinary accomplishments are realized when opportunity meets preparation, and she was undeniably competent to take them on, but she will need help.

Onyx pulled her mask down. It smelled like gas. She turned the corner and saw two fire trucks indicating a gas leak.

Pulling up the mask, she leaned on the side of the building and heard a firefighter instructing people to go back in. "All clear. You folks can get back home," he said to the crowd of people standing outside.

It was dark and cold for early fall. The sky was cloudy, and everyone hurried back in. She watched them. They looked like sheep going about without question. No one asked what had happened, why the smell. No, that's not what sheep do. They follow the herd, doing what they're told. They trust blindly.

That's human nature, and it doesn't matter how awful things may seem, how hopeless or desperate. Everyone wants to turn a blind eye; not their monkey or zoo. So, no one picks up the bucket unless his house is on fire. The rest can burn.

It's about comfort and security. People don't like to be inconvenienced or bothered by thoughts. Most are so absorbed with idle thinking, wasting valuable energy on trivialities, that anything outside of that is frightening.

Humans are selfish, self-centered, and consumed with themselves alone. No one worries about the whole or the bigger picture.

Will they like me?

Am I too fat?

Am I skinny enough?

I'm depressed.

The list is endless. They are all disconnected from one another, convinced that someone else will handle it, the government will solve that problem, science will resolve that other difficulty, and the financial institutions will find a resolution to that crisis, but not me.

While consumed with my difficulties, I cannot entertain those issues, and on closer inspection, they are the product of their choices, as most human troubles usually are.

Turning a blind eye to things that affect the whole often contributes to our issues. Those are Onyx's thoughts and feelings and the probable reason she feels alienated from everyone else.

She waited a few more minutes until the trucks were gone and the last person was inside. There were fire escapes on the backside. She used that as a means of getting into Mateo's apartment.

Onyx tried to open the window to his apartment, but it was locked. *Of course, it's locked. He is very cautious. He checks the stove, the windows, and the door before bed,* she thought, shaking her head.

She couldn't see inside with drawn curtains, so she knocked several times on the window instead. Nothing happened, so she began to head down.

"Onyx?" she heard a voice and looked up, and to her relief, it was a shirtless Mateo.

Quickly, she climbed up and in through the open window. "You know there's a door, right?" he asked, looking at her inquisitively and clutching the towel around his waist.

PART THREE

Identifying people is impossible without facial recognition software, and even then, it is a challenge. It would not be possible if it weren't for the black ops Snap project.

Fortunately, deliberately planning everything in a sequence was genius. As a result, the release of the Snap program was long before they had people in a mask.

That plan was to have people upload photos with every filter imaginable. Overlooking nothing, women used male filters and vice versa. They even had baby filters. It is hard determining someone's age these days. Botox and fillers have everyone looking young, if that's what you can call it.

Kyle had spent hours looking through footage, but everyone looked similar, wearing those silly face masks. A woman wearing a hat and sunglasses caught his eye, but it seemed she was dodging cameras because he didn't see much of her or where she was going, just a brief stop at a food cart not far from the abandoned building. He would probably go there himself to question the vendor.

He received her military file. There was an address listed in the Bronx. He would follow up on every lead. He was still waiting for more information from her childhood. There had to be something, *someone* he could question.

All feedback was negative. The boots on the ground were coming back empty-handed. Finally, Kyle pulled up to the corner where the food cart was.

It was a sunny day, unseasonably warm, and Kyle hated it. He felt himself starting to perspire and wiped the sweat from his forehead as he fought the urge to shove the people in front of him out of the way, but instead, he patiently waited. As soon as he walked up, he showed the man a picture of Onyx.

"Do you remember this person?" Kyle asked, but the man barely looked at it and shook his head.

Kyle pulled out a gun and pointed it at him. "Look at it again. Take your time, and what's with the stupid hat? It's not even that cold yet," he bullied the man. *I'm here sweating, and this dumbass is wearing a fucking hat*, he thought angrily.

By now, the vendor was trembling with fear. "Sir, I apologize, but I see many people daily. So, most of the time, I don't look up. Instead, I listen to the order and quickly prepare, collect the payment, and move on to the next person. So unless they're regulars, it's impossible to remember," he nervously said.

Kyle glared at him, instinctively knowing he was right. He didn't expect her to come to make his acquaintance with a memorable conversation.

Fucking bitch, where are you? he thought as he holstered his gun.

Kyle began to walk, looking around. A train station was nearby, but he had combed through all recordings within the transit system, and after her initial escape, there was nothing conclusive.

He doubted she had used the trains as a means of transportation. The transit system has the most sophisticated surveillance system. Police robots patrol the platforms, basically giant cameras that can use force when necessary. She was lucky to have avoided one of them during her escape.

He had people perusing leads of persons that fit her general description. It was like looking for a needle in a haystack. And the longer it took to locate her, the slimmer the chance of catching her. Kyle was deeply frustrated. He hated that anyone could outsmart him—*especially* Onyx Pion.

They should've killed her the day she took off. That was the time to catch and kill her; now, it seemed highly improbable. He paced back and forth. If she walked, where to?

He looked up the address from the Bronx. "Fucking bitch. It's a damn school!" he shouted, taking out his phone. "Hey, did you get the rest of her file? I need her last address," he said, irritated. He rubbed his temple with his free hand.

"She was in foster care. We're waiting for a list of the homes she was in until she enlisted," Steve told him.

Kyle pressed his lips tightly, trying to contain his anger. "As soon as you get it, forward it," he demanded, ending the call.

It was chilly, but it felt like ninety degrees to Kyle. He despised this ugly city. The stench of it made his stomach turn. He watched the zombielike addicts walk around. They lived on the street, unable to make curfew in the green zones.

The system had failed. However, those on drugs can freely use and live on the street unbothered. That was the fair aspect of the deal.

Onyx ogled Mateo's still-moist body. *Look at those strong muscles and six-pack. He isn't skipping the gym*, she thought, staring at him.

"I wanted to surprise you," she said, looking around and absentmindedly playing with the keys on the table.

He wasn't buying it. That's not Onyx's style. She isn't into surprises or melodramatics. Her visit was about something else.

She looks good, Mateo thought, looking at her ass. Onyx was in the best shape of her life.

"What's going on? Onyx, this isn't like you. I haven't seen you since you started working for that security company about four years ago. What's up?" he asked her, suspicious.

She had been missing in action and showed up unannounced, using the window. It insulted Mateo's intelligence, and he wanted answers.

Sure, I work long hours and have no days off, but I send him a text checking up now and then, she thought. Instead, however, she sensed resentment in his voice.

"Mat, I've been super busy. They work us to the ground … long hours, no days off. But you know I like to keep busy, so I don't mind. I don't have time for anything else," she said nervously.

His apartment was just as she remembered, a small one-bedroom place. The kitchen, dining, and living room were all one ample space.

He had a gray dining table with two chairs, a navy love seat with a small coffee table, and a small bookcase. Mateo loved to read.

He knew her and was sure something was very wrong.

"They have labor laws against shit like that," he said, trying to lighten the mood and break the ice. Onyx gave him a light chuckle.

"I worry about you, kid. But you don't have to treat me like a stranger. You can take a day from your busy schedule to catch up in person, not disappear for years and then show up at my window like a thief in the night," he told her, pained.

Before staring at her feet, she looked him in the eyes. "I'm in trouble," she whispered.

He grabbed her shoulder, gently lifting her chin to meet his gaze.

"What do you mean you're in trouble? Did you get evicted? Did you lose your job? Are you pregnant?" he asked, stepping back to take a better look at her.

She shoved his bare chest. "No, silly, not *that* kind of trouble. I'm in more of a 'people are trying to kill me' kind of a mess," she said and let out a nervous laugh.

"Are you fucking serious? You're kidding me, right?" Mateo asked and frowned, hoping she would say she was joking and announce she was getting married or something of that nature. *Although people trying to kill her sounds more likely than the former*, he told himself.

"I wish I were," she replied, slumping onto the couch. It smelled like cinnamon. It must be the candle on the table. The sofa hugged her, and she felt safe for the first time in a long time. The fear of the threat still pulsed through her veins it was not the kind of safety one required while running for their life. But it was a different sort of security. It was an assurance that she would be OK.

That's the thing with humans. No matter how well we fare on our own, we still need those connections. We need the sanctuary that someone to depend on provides.

Mateo sat on the couch beside Onyx. She rested her head on the back of it and stared at the ceiling. He took her hand and watched her, mesmerized. Her dark chocolate skin, smooth and radiant, was delectable.

"I don't know what kind of clusterfuck you've gotten yourself into and trust me, you'll be telling me all about it, but you look like you need some sleep, so I'll make you some dinner and a hot cup of tea, and we can discuss it tomorrow," he told her.

Onyx looked over at him and wondered what his parents were like, what type of childhood he had survived, or if he always felt safe and loved? Growing up on survival and growing up on love separated people and made them different breeds. That is rarely pondered and yet, makes a difference because a person's upbringing affected how they related to others.

"You know what else I need?" she asked while pulling the towel from his waist.

Mateo chuckled, knowing what she meant, and slowly ran his finger through her curly black hair as she worked her way down to his groin.

Kyle received the list; her last known foster home was in Washington Heights. He rushed there. He was eager to have something tangible. He was so sick of coming up with nothing, and for the first time, he felt hopeful.

A disheveled lady with tangled hair and a dirty pink robe answered the door. "I don't foster kids no more, so get the fuck out," she said, trying to close the door, but Kyle pushed the door in, causing her to stumble backward.

"What the fuck is your problem? My husband works for the city. I'm not squatting here," she said defensively.

"Sorry, Ms. Perez, that's not why I'm here, and frankly, I don't care that you're in this dump," he said, walking past her into the filthy apartment.

"How the fuck are you just gonna walk in here like you own the place?" she asked rhetorically, giving him a death stare.

Kyle pushed clothes off a chair and sat at the dining table, lighting a cigarette. "Please sit," he said, pointing at a chair.

The place reeked of cat piss, tobacco, and stale beer.

"Comes in my goddamn house and dares to tell me to sit the fuck down. Man, what the hell do you want? I'm binging a show," she told him.

"Onyx Pion, you fostered her a few years," he said, getting straight to the point.

He was as eager to get through this as she was for him to leave, although he hoped she irritated him enough so that he could kill her on his way out.

"Who?" she asked, looking confused. "You're here about some kid I fostered? But, man, listen, I don't remember the names of those little motherfuckers, and lastly, I was drunk most of the time," she told him, amused.

Now, she was laughing hysterically. "The only reason I ain't drunk right now is that I just got up, so how about you get the fuck outta my place, so I can get my fucking day started?" she urged.

Two cats jumped on the table hissing, and Kyle shoved them off. *I fucking hate cats*, he thought.

Kyle sighed; she had exhausted his patience sooner than he had anticipated. He pulled out his gun and placed it on the table before him. Then before he reached into his jacket pocket for the silencer, he took the cigarette from between his lips and put it out on her table, burning through the cloth.

"Motherfucker, are you crazy?" she screeched, inspecting the damage, unbothered by the gun. Instead, she was hovering, glaring at him.

"Sit the fuck down," he said, turning the silencer in the gun's muzzle, "or I'll fucking shoot you," he instructed.

Unfazed and still watching him with disdain, she sat. "This place is a fucking pigpen, and you're worried about a stupid tablecloth?" he asked disgustedly.

She rolled her eyes at him. "You need to mind your goddamn business," she mumbled.

"Now, Ms. Perez, let's try this again. Onyx Pion!" he said, the gun pointed at her.

She gave him the finger. "Listen, crazy son of a bitch. Do you think I'm playing with you? I'm a fucking drunk and don't give a rat's ass about none of the little brats that have passed through here. So, you'll have to show me a picture or something, because I don't know who the hell you talking about. The checks came in my motherfucking name. That's all I cared about, and that's all I remember," she told him, exasperated.

He knew she was telling the truth. Empty beer and liquor bottles littered the place, and she was not all there. He lit another cigarette and held it between his lips while reaching into his jacket pocket for the picture he had taken from her military file. Onyx was younger, and he hoped she would remember it as if her life depended on it … because it did.

He slid the photo across the table without speaking. Mrs. Perez reached for it and examined it briefly. "Oh, this little ho had a nasty attitude. I called that one 'Your Highness' because she walked around like she was better than everyone, always mumbling shit under her breath," she told him, pushing the picture back to him.

"She was a weird-ass, introverted kid, had no friends, and didn't go nowhere. I always told her to get out of the house, go some damn place, but she just locked herself in the room. I only saw her listening to the pastor lady from the church downstairs. She ain't talk much, probably due to her little foul attitude," she added.

He put the photo away. "Do you recall anything else?" Kyle asked.

She rolled her eyes again. "That's all I got, you dumb mother—" He shot her in the face before she could finish the sentence.

"You talk too much, lady," he said to her lifeless body slumped over, blood soaking the tablecloth on the table.

The two cats jumped on the table, sniffing the blood. "I hope you're hungry," Kyle said as he left her apartment.

Onyx woke up disconcerted. She had not had a decent night's sleep in days.

Mateo was snoring next to her. *Damn, I probably shouldn't have done that,* she thought as she gently crept out of bed and went to shower.

The bathroom was small and plain. The white subway tiles annoyed Onyx. Still, the hot water felt good, like it decontaminated her, cleansing all the horrible things she had experienced, washing away the pain, the uncertainty, the fear, the frustration, the anger, and the sadness.

"This has to be a dream. I'm dreaming," she said as the water soaked her thick hair and her muscles began to relax.

Water had a soothing effect. Whether swimming in the ocean, a river, a lake, bathing, or showering, it's a symbolic ritual that purifies a troubled soul.

She was there a long time, and Mateo finally interrupted her meditative state. "Don't wash away in there. Breakfast is getting cold," he announced.

Yes, she wished she could dissolve, drift down the drain like water, and disappear into oblivion. But instead, Onyx raised her head into the water and allowed it to fall on her face awhile longer before shutting it off. Then, she wiped the excess water away with her hands, taking a deep breath, inhaling deeply through her nose, and exhaling through her mouth.

A new day was here, full of possibilities, one foot in front of the other. But first, she had to tell Mateo what was going on. She wasn't sure how he would react, but he was wise, and she was confident he would have something enlightening to say that would help her formulate some plan to help keep her alive.

She put on a pair of his boxers and a T-shirt. The scent of crispy bacon, eggs, and syrup was delightful. Onyx realized how hungry she was and hurried to the kitchen. She couldn't recall her last full meal, and her mouth watered at the sight of the food on the table.

Mateo was already sitting down, sipping coffee, but had not touched his food. "Finally, woman. You know you can't wash your troubles away," he said.

She was aware of that, but how she wished she could. She didn't regret what she'd done. She only hoped she had the strength to see it through.

Onyx sat across from Mateo at the small dining table, but at that moment, it felt like the banquet hall of a palace. Sometimes, it's not where you are but who you are with that matters. She realized then that she had missed him. She missed whatever it was they had.

They ate in silence. Onyx felt him watching her eat, but she didn't care. She was too hungry. Fortunately, she wasn't a shy eater.

"That was delicious!" she triumphantly exclaimed after eating as though she had just won first prize in an eating competition.

Mateo laughed loudly. "Damn, girl, when was the last time you ate?" he asked.

He couldn't help recalling all the wonderful times they'd spent in his apartment, and now, everything between them felt formal and awkward, even after what had happened last night.

"Not exactly sure," she said, holding the coffee mug and sniffing the sweet aroma before drinking it.

"If you want more, I can make seconds," Mateo said, unsure that he had given her enough.

"No, thanks. I'm satisfied," she said, patting her stomach.

He smiled at her, relieved. "Good because we have to talk," he said thoughtfully.

PART FOUR

Kyle walked out of the building and lit another cigarette. He stood there looking around, watching people aimlessly walk to and from nowhere. It finally felt like autumn. He welcomed the chill in the air and felt invigorated as if he were one step closer to catching his prey.

He would find Onyx Pion if he had to set this city and the world on fire. Then, adjacent to the building entrance, Kyle saw the church entry. He finished up the cigarette and went in.

The lighting inside the church was poor. With energy prices so high and churches no longer had the luxury of tax exemptions, it was a mystery to Kyle how this place was operational. In addition, religion had an undesirable designation as misogynistic, racist, and not inclusive.

He thought no one was there for a second until he heard someone speak. "Hello, welcome. What can I do for you?" So asked a tall, older man wearing a decrepit gray suit and walking up to him, extending his hand.

Kyle reached out and shook the man's hand. "How do you do?" he asked mockingly, sounding eloquent.

The pastor studied him longer than Kyle was comfortable, so he rudely jerked his hand back and wiped it on his pants as though he had a contagious disease. However, knowing what he knew, his fear was not misplaced.

"The old lady around?" he asked crudely, assuming he was the pastor and keeper of that holy hellhole.

The pastor was still carefully observing Kyle. "I just got back from the airport. My wife's sister is ill, so she went to be with her. Is there anything I can help you with?" he asked, raising an eyebrow.

Travel was exclusively restricted. It was difficult for "regular folks" to purchase a ticket nowadays. Moreover, a person must satisfy specific conditions to fly. For example, his sister-in-law must need someone to care for her, granting his wife permission to travel.

Kyle retrieved the photo from his pocket, ensuring the gun was visible. "You know this person?" he asked, handing him the photograph of Onyx.

Kyle looked at the church, benches pokey and uncomfortable looking. The pulpit stood on cinder blocks. Paint peels, broken light fixtures, and a disgusting moldy smell filled the air.

The pastor took the photograph Kyle gave to him and carefully looked at it. He even turned his head from side to side as he examined it.

"I'm afraid not, young man. I remember everyone who attends or has attended this congregation. So, naturally, I pray earnestly for them. But, unfortunately, I don't recall seeing that young lady here," he informed Kyle calmly.

Kyle reached out for the picture as the pastor handed it back. "She lived in this building here," Kyle said, pointing to the wall next to him.

Onyx was not the religious type, but if they knew something about Onyx, Kyle would find out.

"I see. My wife is very good with people. She strives to reach as many souls as possible, and what better way than to reach out to the community we serve? She probably knows the young lady and invited her countless times," he says, smiling and nodding.

Kyle clenched his fist. *Useless, just like this fucking church he runs*, he thought, annoyed.

"We do God's work, son, but beyond inviting those in the community to come to hear his message and pray for them, there's not much we can do," he added.

God's work? Old fool. I do God's work, Kyle thought. He looked at the pastor, aggravated. "What would the old lady tell me? Because it's urgent I find this girl," Kyle stated.

"That's what she would tell you—everything I've just said. I hope you find what you are looking for. God loves all his children, son, yourself included," he said to Kyle warmly.

Kyle knew he was sincere but still wanted to punch him in the face. "You're wasting your time here, Padre. We are all going to hell, yourself included," he yelled back as he walked out of the church.

Kyle felt anger raise its ugly head, like a foreign entity with its hands around his neck and fangs piercing his flesh, draining any joy in him.

"Are you out of your damn mind?" Mateo shouted as he stood with his hands grasping his head, pacing back and forth across the room. "What the fuck were you thinking? You're not in a movie, not a superhero. You're in *real fucking life*!" he yelled at Onyx.

Now he was standing directly in front of her, absolutely livid. "I cannot believe how naïve you are, Onyx. I bet you have convinced yourself that somehow, you will make the world a better place," he told her angrily.

"Oh, fuck you, Mateo! I'm sorry you don't believe these bullshit vaccines are transgenic substances with the pretense of preventing viruses. A solar simulator, patent US3247367A. Yeah, I know. I'm fucking crazy memorizing patents and shit or for saying that mind-controlling chips and every other nefarious conspiracy theories are true!" She was screaming at him, and he sat on the floor and placed his hands on her knees.

Mateo looked into her big, beautiful brown eyes, "Do you comprehend the severity of what you've done? You're rambling like a crazy person," he told her gently.

She held his gaze for a while. She knew he was upset because he cared about her, and maybe it was selfish of her to think that he would also want to risk his life to expose this.

"I understand that you believe all this is wrong, and somehow you have a duty to tell the world the truth, but I think we all subconsciously know all this to be true. We have collectively allowed it to happen. We are all responsible for our current existence, and I believe it's too late to undo it." Mateo told her that the only thing left was to create something new.

She jumped out of her seat, "What does that mean? What new-age bullshit is this? *Who* are you?" she asked, visibly frustrated.

What did he mean? Am I just supposed to allow the evil powers that be to control, lie, and deceive me? Wait! Was he implying that I am supposed to like *it?* she thought and went into the room and began to dress.

Mateo followed her. "What are you doing?" he asked, concerned.

She turned to face him. "I'm getting dressed to get the fuck out of here! *That's* what I'm doing," she barked at him.

He watched her as she angrily dressed. He sat on the bed, hoping that she would calm down. He wasn't going to say anything else that could trigger her. He understood that she was experiencing post-traumatic stress, that what she had been through was horrible, and that her shock had probably not fully registered the events. She is still in fight mode.

Onyx had been in fight mode since he first met her. It pained him to know that there had never been a time in her life when her guard was down and her defenses weren't active. How can anyone live like that? How does one nervous system survive that?

The irony is she didn't have to tell him. She never talked about anything, but he knew. It's a mystery how you meet people and instantly know them or rather can "see" them, the essence that is them. That's how Mateo felt about Onyx. She didn't have to confide in him. She didn't have to tell him it's been rough. He already knew it.

Once she finished dressing, he stood up and hugged her. She tensed up, trying to get out of the embrace.

"It's OK," Mateo whispered and softly caressed her hair.

This act wasn't a lover's embrace. Instead, this was another human being showing empathy, compassion, and love in a way most people could not demonstrate.

Mateo was in tune with Onyx in a very intimate way. He understood what she felt. He knew Onyx needed him, that she was alone, and that she was trying to survive—not only from this mess she was in but in general.

In its authentic expression, love was a recognition of oneself in another. It was an unconditional acceptance of a person as they are.

Mateo disagreed with what she had done, but he understood that she felt that what she did was the right thing to do at the time, and he would stand with her, not only because she needed him but because he wanted to.

Kyle sifted through papers on his desk, going through every detail. Onyx was utterly alone. "Teachers!" he cried out. *Don't they always try to help the helpless?* he thought.

His teachers always thought they could help him, like something was wrong with him. But of course, there was nothing wrong with him. He felt perfect, like he'd have the world in the palm of his hand one day.

"Losers always want you to be like them," he would tell his mother whenever he got in trouble at school.

He believed the mediocre didn't understand those meant for greatness and therefore always tried to convince them that they were damaged somehow when the reality is they were free to express who they indeed were.

Kyle would track down every teacher, anyone who could have helped her directly or indirectly. He continued scrutinizing every document.

"That's it! A recruiter. How did she get into the military? Who recruited her?" he shouted to the empty office desk in complete disarray.

He was now on his feet, circling his desk, chewing his thumbnail, eyes empty.

Kyle was so consumed with hatred that he would do whatever it took to find Onyx.

People who are entitled and accustomed to getting what they want despised anyone who dared reject them. Unfortunately, Kyle's hatred of Onyx represented just that.

He sent text messages and emails to Steve and associates so that they could locate teachers and her recruiter. But unfortunately, anxiety was crippling him while he waited. He felt sharp pains in his stomach and sat down to calm himself, and he felt his leg shaking involuntarily. Hatred is like poison, and the person who feels it expects the person they hate to be the one who dies.

The phone vibrated in his hand, and he fumbled with it as he answered. "Yeah?" he said, grabbing a pen and scribbling an address on the back of an unopened piece of mail. "Got it," he said, ending the call.

Kyle looked at the address on the paper and entered it into the map application on his phone. Then he hurried out to the location.

It was an apartment building in a still-decent area. Unfortunately, the city was such a shithole now that most facilities were repulsive. The good thing was he had a gun and was not afraid to use it.

Kyle ran up the stairs, and when he finally came to a black door with a gold number 36 on it, he was out of breath, so he rested his arm on the wall, gathering himself before knocking. He took one last big breath, then banged on the door.

"Yes, can I help you?" someone asked.

Kyle didn't like that he came to the door and spoke through a crack with a chain secured to it.

"Good morning," Kyle said, flashing some federal credentials no one could have had the time to see. "I'd like to ask you a few questions," he insisted.

Mateo tilted his head to the side, looking better at Kyle. "Bro, I have somewhere to be. As you can see, I haven't finished dressing," he said, still in his boxers. "I don't know who the local drug dealers or pimps are, so you have a nice day," he said to Kyle.

Before he could shut the door, Kyle pushed it. "That's not why I'm here. Can I come in so we can sit to discuss it?" he asked, visibly frustrated and agitated.

"Look, bro, you look crazy," Mateo said, shaking his head. "What is it you want? Make it quick because time is money," he said.

Kyle wore a black suit with a black shirt, but Mateo found the black tactical boots unusual. One had to notice the minor details.

Kyle wiped the sweat from his brow and let out a sigh. His irritation was palpable. "Look, guy, I'm looking for someone. I believe you recruited her—"

Mateo cut him off. "You're going to have to do better than that. I'm the best recruiter in the region. I recruit, get my money, and keep it moving," Mateo said proudly.

They stared at each other. Mateo stood assertively. What he said was true. If he were looking for someone Mateo had recruited, he would have to be more specific.

Kyle went into his jacket pocket and pulled out a photograph. He handed it to Mateo. "Her name is Onyx Pion. Do you remember her?"

Mateo took the photo and looked at it carefully. She was very young here, the innocence lingering in her eyes, but the countenance of pain was more apparent in the photograph.

Although she appeared wounded, she also exuded strength. That attracted Mateo to her, what drew him into Onyx Pion's orbit.

"So, do you remember her or not?" Kyle asked, bringing him out of his reverie.

"Vaguely. She was cute but fucking weird. But as I said, recruit, get paid, and move on to the next. Was that all?" Mateo said quickly, looking him in the eyes.

Honesty is good at helping one keep their composure, and he answered the question truthfully. Onyx was cute and weird back then and still is, but Mateo was eager for Kyle to leave. Further questioning could make things awkward.

Kyle took the photo and handed him a card. Mateo took it. It had the Orion logo, a name, Kyle Burns, and a number. That's it. "If you remember anything else, give me a call," Kyle said.

Mateo waited for him to clear the stairs before shutting the door, thinking Kyle couldn't be much older than he was, but he appeared older. He was a large man, tall and muscular, with a gut. His eyes were blue, and he had dark reddish hair and a face full of freckles.

Kyle walked down the stairs slowly as he lit a cigarette. He knew Mateo had told him the truth. He was, in fact, the best recruiter in the region, but there was something about him that Kyle didn't like. Maybe it was the cockiness. Kyle didn't like being challenged and hated feeling like others weren't intimidated by him, and Mateo dared to insult him and call him crazy.

Who the fuck does he think he is? he thought. "I should've kicked that fucking door in his face, fucking prick," he said aloud.

He looked in his phone for the addresses of the teachers he had gotten. Then he got in the car and made a call. "Hey, I want someone at an address I'm going to send you; sending a picture too. Keep a close eye on him. I want to know everything he does. I want to know everything he eats, where the asshole goes, and who he sees. If it gets boring, kill him," Kyle ordered.

Onyx was fully dressed, wearing one of Mateo's white T-shirts and the black jeans she had when she arrived. Her gun was in her hand when Mateo entered the room.

They stared at each other without uttering a word. Then Mateo quietly dressed in jeans, a black hoodie, a baseball hat, and boots.

He grabbed a go-bag from the closet filled with his documents, money, MREs, water, weapons, ammunition, and other survival items.

There's no way she's going to make it alone, he thought.

Onyx walked over and grabbed his hand, shaking her head. He knew what she was attempting to convey, but he was all in. He wouldn't let her run alone, especially after meeting the piece of shit who was after her.

He pulled her in by her waist and kissed her. He would follow her to the ends of the earth. He pointed at the window and a number on his watch, then touched his penis and winked at her. She smiled and nodded, understanding what he meant.

They didn't want to speak, afraid that Kyle had deployed spy bugs that could amplify low-decibel sounds and hear their conversation.

Those things can be any tiny insect engineered to record and listen and fit under the door crack.

Mateo didn't know how much Kyle knew, but if special detection drones weren't already hoovering outside the building, they would be soon. Those can detect heat signatures in dwellings and would quickly know two people were in his apartment. Kyle didn't ask if Mateo was alone, but they had to leave because his apartment was compromised.

The meeting place would be the library where they had sex for the first time. Mateo was helping Onyx fill out some applications, explaining basic training, and discussing books. He had asked if she had read *The Alchemist*, and she said no, so they went to find it.

The library was nearly empty, and he saw an open closet in a dark corridor and pulled her in. He just wanted to kiss her, but they got carried away, and it was an exhilarating experience they both recalled fondly.

Mateo wanted Onyx to be his girlfriend, but he didn't dare ask because she was constantly emotionally unavailable. "We are special friends, nothing more, so don't get any ideas," she said once they were out of that closet, shattering Mateo's heart.

Mateo walked out of the building and quickly surveyed his environment. He was familiar with the area because he was a longtime resident and trained himself to be conscious of his surroundings.

Most people spend their lives on autopilot and only pay attention to tasks when they are engaged in them for the first time. Then they return to the autopilot setting, getting carried through life as a leaf carried by the wind.

He was heading to the office. He would finish some paperwork for a recruit, make a few calls, stay there a few hours, and then leave to catch up with Onyx.

They had no means of communication. Onyx didn't have a cell phone because it would be too easy to track, so they had agreed that she would call him at the office in case of an emergency.

Mateo wrote Onyx a note with the office number and other instructions. He wished she would stick to the plan. However, Onyx could be unpredictable, and he feared she would leave without him.

Mateo had a plan, something he was arranging before she came back into his life. He felt this was fate, like she came back with this apparent problem because they had to leave everything behind together.

Being a hopeless romantic was not something he thought would ever describe him. Still, the more he thought about the situation, the more he noticed his behavior and recognized that it was a very accurate description. *I love her*, he thought. It was the first time he admitted those feelings to himself, and he smiled. He realized that the best part of himself had manifested at that moment.

Love can make people do crazy things. But hopefully, this isn't something he will regret later.

He reached the train station and ran down the stairs. Suddenly, he stopped. There was another staircase directly across from where he had entered the station. Mateo ran over and went up halfway. Then he sat on a step looking at the stairs on the other side when suddenly, a guy ran down that caught his eye.

Mateo was sure he caught a peripheral glimpse of him walking parallel to him across the street. He observed him subtly looking around as though he was looking for someone. *He's following me*. Mateo was sure of it.

The guy disappeared into the crowd toward the turnstiles. If he were following him, he would keep a distance, confident that Mateo would not notice and expect to find him at the turnstile landing, either looking for access on his mobile or just getting onto the platform.

A police robot looked over at Mateo, and he stiffened. Photos of wanted persons were sent to the robots daily, and Mateo didn't know if Orion knew that Onyx had been with him. Slowly, Mateo stood and concealed himself behind a wall. Then, to his relief, the robot moved on.

Mateo waited a few more minutes to see if this guy was still following him because not finding him where he calculated would force him to double back ... and he did. Mateo observed him look over to the staircase where he was hiding, so he stealthily walked up the stairs and back in the direction of his building.

He stopped at a deli a block away, bought bottled water, and looked out the window to see if he saw him, and there he was, on the corner on his phone. Mateo decided that he would go back to his apartment.

Every action requires a logical explanation, so he instantly decided that he would explain his behavior with something rational and indisputable, like he forgot his wallet somewhere. Once he was confident that his tail was gone, he returned home.

ANAMNESIS

Onyx's contract was up. So, after four years in the military, she finally returned to New York.

"Hey, Mateo," John from the deli near his apartment said when he saw him. He'd been living around here his whole life.

"What's up, John?" I said, placing the beers on the counter.

"Same old crap; taxes went up again. If they keep it up, I won't be in business for much longer," John complained.

"I hear you, my brother," I told him. It will suck if this place goes under too.

"Are you having a party, or are you trying to keep cool?" he asked.

"Yeah, it's freaking hot, but my friend is coming to visit," I said.

"The pretty girl that you come in here with sometimes?" he asked, referring to Onyx.

"Yes, she's returning from the service," I said.

"Cool, well, you have a nice rest of your day," John said as I left.

"Thanks."

I prepared chicken, rice, and beans, with a green salad. I hoped she liked it. She always complained about the food when she came to visit.

I heard a knock on the door and ran to open it.

"My God, it's hot out there. New York weather is so extreme," Onyx said, walking into my apartment. She only had a carry-on and a backpack.

"Welcome back," I said. I wanted to say "home," but I didn't want to make her uncomfortable.

Onyx said she needed to crash at my place until she got on her feet, and when I told her my home was her home, she got upset.

"No, that's *your* home. You're a great friend, and I don't plan on intruding long," she told me. "But thanks, M&M" she said.

"You look good," I said, and it was true. Onyx wore light blue jeans that hugged her amazing ass perfectly and a white tank top with no bra. Her perky breasts looked delicious.

"You hungry?" I asked, walking off, so she didn't notice my excitement.

"Always," she replied, following me.

She sat at the small dining table, and I served her dinner. "It smells great," she said with a smile.

"I hope you like it," I told her.

"You've always been a great cook," she reminded me.

"I'll go put your bags in the room," I said, walking away.

She's the hottest girl I've ever seen, but I'm not sure what Onyx I'm getting. The "friends only" or the "friends with benefits."

Sadly, I can't say "girlfriend" because that's not an option. I can only leave the ball in her court, but I will always be whatever Onyx Pion needs me to be.

"You not eating?" I heard her call out.

"Yes, I am," I said as I joined her.

"I'll take some more so that you don't have to eat alone," she said, handing me an already-empty plate.

"Wow, impressive," I said with a smile.

That night, I was happy to know she had returned as my "friend with benefits." In fact, she ravaged me all night, and I was happy as fuck.

The next couple of weeks were frustrating for Onyx. She couldn't find a decent job, and I could sense her disappointment. She complained that she couldn't live with me forever and that she was cockblocking any girl from dating me.

I wanted to tell her that the only girl I wanted to date was her, but I knew that would push her away.

"We can enjoy each other's company while we have it," I told her, going under the sheets and pulling her shorts down.

"I'm serious," she protested, but my tongue had already found the sweet spot, and she lay her head on the pillow without further objection.

Living with Onyx was easy. We didn't argue. We had fun. She is the chill friend you can talk to, with sex being the bonus, although often, she goes cold. I knew she didn't want to be bothered or spoken to, so I just left her alone those times.

Finally, she got a job with Alpha, a security company. She hated it but kept it until she could build a résumé and find something better. Onyx wanted the top dog, Orion, but one can spend years waiting to hear from them, and their selection and hiring process was grueling.

They can dismiss you right out of training. Although I didn't think that would happen with Onyx, getting her foot in the door was what worried me.

After three months, she left Alpha and went to work for Orion's competitor, Prime Security.

"Hey, I just found out my buddy's uncle works for Orion. Do you want me to ask him to help you get in?" I asked Onyx one night when she had gotten home from work.

"I appreciate it, Mat, but I want to get in on my own. I know I can. I only have to wait for them to get to my application," she told me.

"OK, but you are overqualified. If Orion doesn't select you, it's their loss," I said to her.

"You know what you can do for me, though?" she asked, pulling down my boxers.

I laughed, immediately hard in anticipation.

"I've been looking for an apartment. The rent is ridiculous, but I think I could manage a small studio with what I've saved. If I get the job with Orion, though, I won't have to worry," she told me.

I turned over to look at her. "Why don't you stay here with me? I don't understand what the problem is. We can be together as a couple, and we get along fine. So why do you act like I'm kicking you out?" I said to her.

"Mateo, we are friends. That's why I need to be in my own space because I don't need you to get any ideas. It would help if you didn't ruin our friendship with your need for a relationship," she said, aggravated.

Is she serious?

"News flash. We are practically in a relationship, sweetheart. Just because you are emotionally unavailable and can't talk about your childhood and why you can't open up doesn't mean this *isn't* a relationship," I replied angrily.

"You're so fucking needy. I'm sorry I'm not good enough, but don't worry. As of right now, we are *only* friends, and I'll be gone real soon," she said, getting up and going to the living room.

I followed her. She lay on the couch, looking up at the ceiling. "You're just right for me. I'm sorry you're not enough for yourself, and yes, I *am* needy. I need to know what you think, how you feel, and why you can't open up to me," I said to her desperately.

"Fuck off, Mateo."

"I know you had a shitty childhood, but you don't need to be a shitty person," I told her.

"Go fuck yourself, Mateo. How's *that* for shitty?" she screamed.

"You're a coward, Onyx! You're scared, afraid of love, of being happy. You're so used to being miserable that anything outside of that scares you," I replied as I walked to the bedroom and left her alone.

After six months in, we had our first fight. After that, Onyx didn't say much for the next few weeks. It was like living with a roommate who hates you. I had told her I would take the couch, but she refused. "You won't be uncomfortable in your place because of me," she told me.

A month later, she came home late, and apparently, she had been drinking. So she came into my room and got in bed with me. Confused, I looked at her, but she went under the sheets and undressed me.

Onyx has her love language, and at that moment, I decided to accept whatever crumbs I could get; maybe I deserved better, but unfortunately, she was what I wanted.

Things got better; she talked to me again, and I was glad. She's funny, and I enjoy her company. She said she would still sleep on the couch, but with her sex drive, she spent most nights in my bed.

"Hey, guess what?" she told me one evening as we ate.

"What?" I asked.

"I heard back from Orion. So I start training next week. If I make it through it, I get the job!" she exclaimed excitedly.

My heart sank to my stomach.

I was happy for Onyx. I want her to be happy and prosperous. I want her to have everything she desires, but I'm sad for myself. I knew she would pass that training and get that job. Then when she did, she would be gone.

"That's great, Onyx. Finally, you'll get what you want," I said, hoping to help her realize maybe she already had it.

"Yes, I can't thank you enough for taking me in. I promise I'll be out of your hair once I finish my training and know I have the job," she said.

I wanted to tell her that I didn't want her to go, that I wanted her to stay with me, and that my world would collapse when she left. But instead, I smiled at her. "It was no big deal. I'm always here for you, kid," I told her.

"I know, and it means the world to me because you're everything I've got. You're my family, M&M, and I'll never be able to repay you," she said, reaching over and taking my hand.

That's the most vulnerable she's ever been and the only time she told me how she felt. You love and care about family, so it felt good.

I nodded and smiled. I wanted to say a million things at that moment, but I was afraid of triggering her.

Onyx wasn't the coward in this equation. I was. She didn't want to be in a relationship with me and told me every chance she got, but I was always too afraid to tell her how I felt all the time she'd been here.

The training was tough. Onyx came home with bruises every day. "God, I'm exhausted," she told me one night as she lay on the couch.

I went over and gave her a foot massage, and when I finished, she came over and kissed me. After that, we had sex on the floor and fell asleep there. Luckily, it was Friday, and we were both off the following day.

"Let's go for a run in Central Park," she told me after breakfast.

"OK, but why don't you take a break? You've been training super hard, and Orion is pushing you to the breaking point," I said to her.

"No way. This jerk at training thinks it's a competition. I want to tell him, 'Dude, I only want to pass to get the job,' but I think it bothers him that I always end up on the top spot," Onyx said.

"Men don't like it when women are better than them, especially in something as physically demanding as that Orion training is," I replied.

"Yeah, I know, but can you believe the asshole asked me to go out for drinks? He called me 'sweet cheeks.'"

I felt instantly jealous and wanted to find and punch him in the face.

"What you say to that?" I asked curiously.

"I told him he was a pig and that I don't go out with losers," she said, laughing.

"Ouch," I said, laughing as well.

"He was furious. After that, he was my sparring partner and came for blood, but he was too slow for me, and that didn't end well for him either. He wound up with a bloody nose," she told me.

"He hates you now for sure, you know," I warned her.

"Yeah, I'll admit my ribs hurt. The loser caught me with a good one. I blocked it, but it was an angry punch," she admitted.

"Well, why don't you invite him over so I can kick his ass and tell him that's no way to get the girl," I told her.

"I can take care of myself, Romeo. Now, let's go," she said.

Onyx finished the Orion training top of her class, and she got the job. To celebrate, we went out to eat. She wore a short black dress with red heels that I wanted to rip off and make love to her instead of leaving the house.

"How do I look?" she asked.

"Like a million bucks," I said, keeping it friendly.

"You clean up nice too," she told me.

I wore all black: slacks, a long-sleeved shirt, a tie, and shoes. Maybe it was symbolic, as if it were a funeral.

She confessed over dinner that she had put down the security deposit for a studio apartment. "The apartment will be ready next week!" she exclaimed excitedly.

"That's great," I said with a smile, attempting to conceal my sadness.

"I couldn't have done this without you, Mat, none of it. It's as much your accomplishment as it is mine. Thank you," she said gratefully.

"I will always be here for you, Onyx. You are my family too," I responded.

Onyx moved, and it didn't hit me immediately because initially, I was helping her assemble furniture, paint, and get her place ready.

After being there late, I spent a few nights, but she hadn't started work at Orion yet. She was now doing a two-week course on company policy. She even had to sign a nondisclosure agreement and see a company doctor, but she didn't give many details.

When she officially started working, things changed. She wasn't a warm and fuzzy ball of light before, and I felt a shift in her personality. She was more distant and closed off than ever.

I barely saw or heard from her. I missed her like crazy and was depressed for a while. "I know we're just friends, but what happened to me being family? Oh, that's right; she doesn't know what that's like," I said bitterly to my empty room after going three weeks without hearing from her.

About two months later, I got a text. "*Hey, Mat, hope all is well. Been super busy with work, it's nonstop, but I love it. Talk to you soon,*" she wrote.

"*Good for you,*" I replied.

After all our time together, Onyx treated me like I was nothing. I'm not even good enough to get a phone call.

As always, I'm a coward and don't say what I genuinely want to say, desperately hoping she will throw some crumbs my way soon.

What I wanted to say was don't text me because you feel obligated, as if you remember, "Oh shit, Mateo. I haven't replied to his phone calls. Let me send him a pity text."

The following year was brutally agonizing without Onyx. Finally, I saw her once over Christmas. She stopped by to give me a gift, a beautiful leather wallet with the initials *M&M* engraved.

She spent the night, we had fantastic sex, and then she disappeared again. So after a while, I stopped calling. Instead, I would reply to her random texts. "*I hope you're doing well,*" and eventually gave up on ever seeing her again.

PART FIVE

Onyx climbed out of the window onto the fire escape. She began to descend but changed her mind. So instead, she went up to the roof and sat there, taking deep breaths. Onyx closed her eyes and continued to breathe consciously.

It's funny. Most people live and aren't aware of it. "Is it worth involving Mateo in this mess?" she asked herself. "Why not just go on the run on my own? It would be easier. How did they come upon Mateo?" she wondered.

Onyx underestimated Kyle. "That piece of shit is relentless."

There was no way this story would have a happy ending. Where will she go? There was no one, not a soul to her name, but Mateo and Alma. It must appear sad, but for her, it was liberating. There was no one to hold her down, nothing to restrict her, no cage to restrain her, no one to answer. She could vanish without owing anyone any explanation. No one would search for her.

How many people live lives they detest because they have children to care for, spouses they are committed to, dependent upon, and to some extent, depend on others for fulfillment and happiness. It is inescapable that we are codependent on each other. Yet, invisible threads connect those meant to be in our lives regardless of their relation.

Onyx is perfect on her own. She has no desire to have another come into her life to complete or make her happy—or the pressure of the expectation that she must provide those things for someone else.

Maybe it's her apathy. She feels somehow she is damaged or somewhat different, unable to connect profoundly or forge meaningful bonds. "I'm selfish. I can't drag Mateo into this, despite him wanting to help me," she said to herself.

Having made up her mind, she rose. She would make a run for it and leave without Mateo. He deserved better than what she was offering. But as is common in this area, the buildings connect, so she jumped to the adjacent roof and went down. Luckily, the roof alarm had been disabled.

The streets were busy with zombielike people, pretending to be aware, but with heads buried in phones, engaged in meaningless conversations, scrolling through social media, listening to music, desperately attempting to escape reality.

Onyx kept looking over her shoulder, ensuring no one was following her.

"What do you mean you lost him? It was a simple fucking task. Follow the fucking guy and let me know every damn thing he does! How hard can it fucking be? Go to the recruiting office where he works, see if he's there, and report back, you idiot." Exasperated, Kyle ended the call.

Where was he headed? Did he know we're following him? How could he? Was there a connection to Onyx? There seemed to be none other than that he was her recruiter. Maybe he was wasting his time on that motherfucker, but he would leave no stone unturned.

Kyle's phone rang. "What is it? Where? How long ago? Is he sure? OK, I'm on my way," he said.

He ran out. An asset was sure he had seen Onyx near Mateo's building. He was following all leads that Kyle had given and was going to his apartment to see if there was anything useful when he saw a woman fitting Onyx's description about a city block away.

Kyle was keen on getting there. He felt a thrill anticipating the torture he would unleash on her. His ire was so intense it aroused him.

"If she gets away from him, I'll kill him where he stands," he murmured, running to his car.

The phone rang again, and he answered via the vehicle's Bluetooth system. "What is it?" he asked, annoyed while driving fitfully.

"Sir, do you want me to engage? I'm following the target now," the asset asked him.

Kyle howled and hit the steering wheel repeatedly because the driver in front slammed on his brakes, causing Kyle to almost crash into him. But instead, he swerved around him and shouted profanities as he sped off.

"Listen to me carefully. Engage only to subdue and restrain. I want that bitch alive. If you lose her, I'll fucking kill you. Am I making myself clear?" he shouted.

Mateo was back in his apartment. He paced back and forth, attempting to calm himself. Should he go to the office as planned or find Onyx? Was he still being followed? Was there a stakeout outside his place? Was Onyx all right? What if they saw her leave, and they got to her?

He never had, in all his life, experienced anxiety like this. It was crippling. He sat down because he felt faint. "What the fuck did I get myself into?" he whispered. "Is it even worth it?" he asked himself.

She had disappeared for years and turned up now with a bounty on her head. Was he going to jeopardize everything for her?

Mateo felt his body answer yes. Too complex to explain, yet every cell in his body screamed *yes* in unison. He went to the refrigerator for some water. He needed to calm himself and formulate a plan. His priority now was to locate Onyx.

He had to get to the library. Mateo went to the window, trying to identify a stakeout or see anything out of the ordinary. "Is that—?" he cut himself off.

Onyx was walking away across the street. She waited, not wanting to leave too soon after he did, which was probably clever because they would have spotted her too.

What if someone is still out there? he thought. He had to get to Onyx. So he ran out, hoping to catch up. As he ran down the stairs, he bumped into someone. "Sorry," he said without stopping to see who it was.

Once outside, he walked casually. If they were watching him, he had to keep cool. He decided to follow Onyx rather than engage. That would be suspicious. He would maintain that he had not seen her. For all he knew, she also lived in the neighborhood. That was a stretch, but it was his story, and he was sticking to it.

Mateo saw Onyx distantly but was afraid to pick up the pace. She was walking fast.

The man Mateo bumped into on his way down was one of Kyle's guys. The one Steve had sent to Mateo's apartment but who then spotted Onyx.

Kyle was now sure Onyx had been with Mateo and wanted irrefutable proof. He wanted DNA from the apartment. He was sure there would be some matching hers and perhaps some clue about their plans.

When Kyle informed Simon of Mateo, Simon told him he couldn't just kill the Golden Boy recruiter without being sure, and now, Kyle hated Mateo just as much and wanted him dead.

"Hey, this guy is running out of his apartment. I thought you said he wasn't there," he said to Steve after seeing Mateo leave.

There was no immediate reply. So, finally, Steve said, "Follow my original instructions. Go to his apartment and get what you can. First, I'll let Kyle know he went back. Then I'll send someone else out to see if they can locate and follow him. We acquired the main target, and Kyle is en route," Steve told him.

The apartment door was ajar. Mateo left hurriedly, so the asset silently entered and locked the door. He immediately noticed two plates and two cups on the table. He took both cups and put them in the backpack he was carrying.

Then he went to the bedroom, opened drawers, and looked through the bookcase. There was no computer. He went through the entire apartment, but there was no sign of what they had planned or where they were going.

If not for the two-place settings on the table, it would appear that he lived alone. There was no indication that he shared the place with a woman. Maybe she had come over for breakfast. He was sure Kyle was going to be furious. The man was off his hinges.

Kyle was unpredictable and had become a liability. Simon planned on "retiring" him once they mitigated this situation.

Steve would rise to take his place. That's the thing about this business: one day, you're on the top of the food chain, and the next, you're dead and replaced.

Onyx was walking fast. *Maybe I should slow down*, she thought. She kept looking over her shoulder, feeling uneasy. She had no plan where she would go. Leaving the state was her best option. However,

Orion had operations across the nation and the globe, so no place was out of its reach.

Maybe her best option was taking a taxi across state lines to New Jersey. Unfortunately, most taxis required customers to swipe a form of identification for access, and paying cash was nearly obsolete. Although the government tracked all transactions so they could collect taxes, those wanting to find a loophole and keep something for themselves accepted cash payments, but it was risky.

The government offered tax breaks to self-employed individuals and businesses that report those who pay cash. Then they follow up by looking into your accounts and placing you under indefinite surveillance. *Equity for all, tax the rich, right?* Onyx thought, looking down the street.

She hailed a taxi and quickly got in. "Hi, how are you doing this morning?" she asked brightly.

"Not bad. How about yourself?" an older man kindly asked.

"Actually," she said with a sad frown, "I lost my wallet and was able to borrow money to make it back home. So is it OK to swipe your ID and accept cash payment?" she asked him sweetly.

He watched her through the mirror. "Well, I don't see why not. Where you headed?" he asked.

You can easily manipulate people when you appeal to them emotionally. That is the weapon of choice of the powers that control the world. They use media to influence the unaware masses emotionally.

Onyx wrote an address on paper and handed it to him. "Wow, that's far. It's going to cost you double, you know?" he said, and she gave him a warm smile.

"That's not a problem, thank you." After that, the ride was mostly silent. The kind gentleman asked a few casual questions, but nothing too intrusive.

Over the years, Onyx slowly withdrew money from her accounts. There is a limit on how much a person can withdraw monthly before being flagged. Five hundred a month, that's it! Of course, you have no control over your own money, but she made sure that she took out the total amount of what was hers each month.

Onyx welcomed the silence while lost in her thoughts. When she was a child, she had gone with a foster mother to visit a relative. The house was small but beautiful, and it impacted her. It was the yard she loved. It had beautiful, lush green grass with a swing set, and a playful golden retriever chased her around. It was the only happy memory she had of her childhood.

Onyx often fantasized about living there with her parents and the siblings she wished she had. They ate delicious meals at the dining table, told jokes, and laughed at her jokes. Those fantasies helped her survive.

It was like having another life she could escape to. She liked to believe it was real. But her actual existence was a nightmare. What if? What if waking is a dream, and our fantasies and sleep state are reality?

Suddenly, an impact threw her across the taxi cabin like a rag doll. She hit her head, and everything went black.

Mateo saw her get into a taxi and frantically stopped one himself. Then, with his identification already in hand, he asked the driver to follow the cab a few cars ahead.

"It's my girlfriend. She forgets everything. She left her keys. I'm heading out of town, and she won't be able to get into the apartment later," Mateo said, and the young man laughed.

"I feel you, brother. My girl leaves her ID everywhere they ask her for it. It's such an inconvenience. So I tell her to tie it around her neck," he said to Mateo.

Where was she going? It wasn't the library. She was running without him. Why didn't she tell him? What was she thinking? And where the fuck was she going? Too many thoughts at once. He felt angry. After everything he was willing to sacrifice for her, *this* is how she repays him.

"What the hell? He's going straight for the—" Before he could finish, Mateo saw a car smash into the taxi Onyx was riding in. It was a deliberate impact on the passenger side. "Shit!" Mateo exclaimed with his hands on his head.

He saw that piece of shit that had gone to his place exiting the vehicle that crashed into her taxi. Mateo pulled out his gun and got out of the cab. Kyle was walking over to open the door, but Mateo took a shot, hitting Kyle in the shoulder. He ducked, and Mateo ran over to the driver's side of the taxi. Onyx was out cold. He shook her.

"Onyx, wake up!" Mateo shouted when a gunshot hit the door. "Shit shit shit!" He took a knee, using the door as cover. There was another shooter. Kyle had retreated to his vehicle. He was probably calling in for backup.

Mateo opened the driver's door, pulled the driver out, and got in. Then, he took off, hitting a few cars and attempting to escape the jam. The taxi's GPS registered an address, but Mateo knew they had to ditch the cab as soon as possible. They all have trackers, but he needed Onyx awake and able to move on foot. If not, they were both dead.

He heard groaning from the backseat. "Good morning, sunshine. Can you walk?" he asked, watching her in the mirror as she sat up, holding her head.

"What happened?" she asked with a grimace.

"I'd like to ask you the same thing. We agreed to meet at the library, but you obviously had other plans, and your buddy caught up to you. The piece of shit thought crashing into you was a good idea. You'd be dead if it weren't for me, but you can thank me later," he said, furious.

Onyx didn't answer, and there was an awkward silence. "Can you walk? We have to ditch this taxi," Mateo asked mechanically.

"Yes," she said somberly. "Look, I'm sorry I was leaving without you, but you deserve better. You don't have to risk your life for me. It's not worth it," she said, rubbing her head.

He turned to face her. "I don't have to do anything, but I *want* to. It was my choice to make, not yours. If you didn't want to involve me in this, you should have stayed away, but you didn't, so now, don't try to choose for me. I also shot your little friend. He looks like he holds a mean grudge, so too fucking late," he shouted angrily.

His words pierced her, and she felt ashamed. Mateo was right. He knew her. Onyx should have never come to him with this problem in the first place. Instead, she only tried to tug at his emotions because she knew she needed him.

She ran without Mateo but wanted him to come after her, and she got what she wanted. She kept away from him all those years, only to come back to ruin his life. She was beyond selfish.

Onyx has dragged Mateo into this mess, and Kyle will not rest until they die.

PART SIX

The crowded border was overwhelming, people shoving and pushing, screaming and demanding to be allowed across. The Florida National Guard was actively engaged and on strict orders of no entry. Ironic how we thought we would create a utopia … only to destroy the fabric of our society.

The propaganda consumed us, and we believed the narratives fed to us, the perfect psych ops, a perfectly executed plan that destroyed the very people they promised equity and fairness to, Onyx thought as she watched.

It was hot. Onyx felt sweat dripping down her back and chest between her breasts. The sun relentlessly blasted them with its rays. It even felt as though the ground was sweating because the humidity was unbearable, made worse by the angry mob.

Mateo had a tight grasp on her hand. His buddy from the marines was now in the Florida Guard and was going to let them through. He had some visas for him and Onyx. Mateo had sent word that he was coming with a plus one, and his buddy arranged for Onyx to receive political asylum.

Unfortunately, they had to fight their way through the desperate multitudes of people urgently attempting to get out of the US.

The fence stretched across the old state line, and a patrol of Florida's armed forces secured it. Once at the gate entrance, Mateo identified himself, and the soldier radioed in. After he had received confirmation that they could pass, the soldier instructed them to enter a tent for a security check. The process was grueling from beginning to end, and getting there was almost miraculous, but they made it alive and, most importantly, together.

After being granted political asylum, members of the Floridian government were interested in meeting with Onyx. Mateo was confident that their interest was the information she had stolen from Pharma Corp. Although Mateo was reluctant to reveal what she had done, he needed leverage to get her entry into the country.

There was no way he would have been able to get her legally into the Republic of Florida without any benefit to the government. Are there any "good guys" when all are only trying to further their agenda?

Mateo wasn't sure that what she had would be helpful to this government, but she was out of the US. There was no way for Kyle to find them here. They were safe, and the possibilities were endless.

Mateo's friend Nathan lives with a community thriving off-grid, living harmoniously off the land, absent from the noise and stress of urban living. Mateo was exhausted and only wanted to disappear into nature and live out the rest of his days peacefully.

He hoped Onyx was willing to join him, but there was a fire burning in her eyes. He could see that the idea of meeting with this government and presenting them with her information gave Onyx renewed hope.

Mateo was unsure of what she hoped to accomplish, but she was verifiably delusional, thinking she could somehow change things and make a difference. He hoped to help her understand that everything in life was about choice. People have chosen and, more importantly, *accepted* everything that has happened.

They welcomed the life they were now living with open arms. Not all, judging by the current state of Florida's border, but that was a minuscule number of the unsatisfied. Mateo believed everything was unfolding as it should and that people were indeed free to choose.

Onyx's insistence on opening people's eyes was futile, for no one can force another to see what they are not prepared to perceive. We can only open our eyes, observe what resonates true in our souls, change our reality, and leave everyone to figure it out for themselves.

They arrived at the hotel, all accommodations courtesy of the Republic.

Onyx began to undress as soon as the room door shut behind them. Clean clothes lay on the bed for them.

"For the love of God, that heat is infernal. It's like literal hell out there. I couldn't breathe, and it's so freaking humid. I can't recall sweating so damn much before in my entire life," she complained as she removed her underwear.

They laughed. "I need a shower immediately. I bet your balls are salty as hell," she said, still laughing, and Mateo pressed his pelvis on her butt as he held her waist.

"Only one way to find out," he whispered in her ear.

She turned to face him with mischief in her eyes and pulled his pants down, holding his gaze.

"You will be my death, woman," he said, closing his eyes in ecstasy.

They went into the shower together. "God, I'm hungry," she said, pouring bath gel into her hands. "I hope the hotel has decent food," she said, lathering her body with soap.

"You just had a mouthful!" Mateo exclaimed, smiling. "You're not easily satisfied, woman," he said, massaging the soap on her back and ass.

He slid his hand across her stomach and down her groin. She was moist with excitement as she turned to find his lips. She passionately kissed him as he continued to rub between her legs, causing her to moan with pleasure.

His hands found her breasts which he gently cupped, licking, and gently sucking each nipple. Exhilarated, she pulled his hair. He made his way down to her dripping wetness, bringing her to climax with his greedy tongue.

Then he lifted her to a straddle and penetrated her with readiness. Her moans intensified his arousal, bringing him to a euphoric state. Finally, she wrapped her legs tightly around his waist, squeezing his pulsating wood in her tight walls.

The water was warm. He continued to thrust fervently inside her, and as her breathing and moaning deepened, he felt like he were on fire. His grip tightened, digging into her backside. She was licking his neck and ear.

He pushed her harder against the wall. Then he took one hand and stimulated her clitoris, causing her to scream. She was swaying up and down, clawing his back with anticipation. "Oh God, I'm comin'!" she cried out, climaxing with him.

The journey there took its toll. They were exhausted physically and emotionally. Mateo was unaccustomed to sharing a bed with anyone, but sleeping beside her gave him comfort and a sense of peace.

The following day, Mateo awoke feeling out of place. "What time is it?" he asked.

Onyx turned to look at the clock on the nightstand. "It's 12:01," she said, raising herself on one elbow as she leaned forward to kiss him lightly.

"Wow, it's been awhile since I slept in so late. But then again, I've never had to run for my life before. That shit was exhausting," he said.

"No kidding," she replied, lying on the pillow and staring at the ceiling.

The white paint had a streak of light glimmering across it. The closed curtains kept the room dark, but that ray of light was coming through a small opening where the two curtain panels met. So even in the darkest hour, we can still see the light if we have hope. *The crack is how the light gets in*, Onyx thought, remembering having read that somewhere.

The room was clean and modestly furnished, with a bed, two nightstands, a desk, and a small refrigerator. She looked at the fridge, thinking how thirsty she was, and closed her eyes again. *What now? What is this with Mateo? What are we going to do?* she thought.

They left everything behind and were now foreigners in this new nation. Would others trust them here? Who's to say they wouldn't kill them once they obtained the information she had promised to supply. What did they plan to do with the information? Going to war was not practical. The US still had superior military capabilities. So, what's the angle?

Onyx's mind was racing. She didn't like the uncertainty. It must be a result of her childhood trauma of constantly having to move around, but for now, they were safe, and she would savor and enjoy each moment. If she had learned anything from her near-death experience, it was that life is short, and most things aren't as serious as we attribute their importance.

Onyx and Mateo spent the next few days in the hotel room, only going out for runs and eating. They worried Orion could track them down here, but Onyx was determined to make the best of it.

"Damn, you're insatiable," Mateo said as she mounted him on the bed and he cupped her breasts.

"And you love it," she replied.

"I'm not complaining," he said excitedly.

The next day, they traveled south to Miami, the nation's capital, and there, they would wait to meet with Mateo's friend, Ivan. He was in the Guard and came for them two days later. They had a meeting with General Jones. Onyx would provide the information in her possession to him.

The general wanted both of them to join their ranks because of their military skills and expertise.

"Did you guys get some rest?" Ivan asked as they followed him to a black SUV parked outside the hotel. He wore his uniform, which Onyx thought was ridiculous but assumed that's what they do here.

"We tried," Mateo said, giving Onyx a flirtatious look.

Onyx did not allow him to rest because having sex was all she wanted to do. And unfortunately, there was not much else they could do.

"Is this all you want me for?" Mateo asked her last night.

"Yes, sir. What else is there to want?" she replied and then promptly fell asleep.

They got into the vehicle. Another gentleman was in the driver's seat. Ivan rode in the back with Onyx and Mateo.

"I understand that you have some valuable information," he said, looking at Onyx. She had not said a word since he arrived. But of course, she was only observing. You can tell a lot about people if you pay attention.

"Yes," she said shortly, looking out the heavily tinted window.

He was only an errand boy. There was no use in discussing things with him. She had learned valuable lessons working for Orion, and speaking with Mateo's friend was a waste of time.

"What is it you do, Ivan?" Mateo asked, attempting to distract from Onyx's rudeness.

"Oh, I'm the first lieutenant. I oversee operations for the general. I'm his right-hand man, mostly in charge of intelligence," he said proudly.

I want to speak to the head, not the hand! Onyx thought and smirked.

"That's awesome," Mateo replied with a genuine smile.

"Yeah, man, you're going to love it here. The Guard is great—no need to be heavy on recruiting. Everyone is eager to serve. You can come work with me at intelligence," Ivan told him.

Onyx looked at Mateo questioningly. He had expressed a ridiculous idea of moving off the grid with what she could only interpret as a new-age cult.

"Nah, buddy, those days are over for me. I only want to chill, enjoy life, and do something different," Mateo told him.

Onyx rolled her eyes. "Like what exactly?" she asked sardonically.

Mateo was annoyed that she would ask him that question in front of Ivan. He knew she felt disdain about him not wanting to join the Guard, but it was none of her business.

"How's the family, Ivan? I bet your baby boy is growing fast. How's Jahaira?" Mateo asked, ignoring Onyx.

Onyx looked out the window, a triumphant grin across her face. *Coward. Why not say what you're planning to your friend? Deep down, you know it's a stupid idea. Why quit and pretend the world is well and disappear into the swamp?* she thought.

Onyx wanted Mateo to put his abilities and intelligence to good use, but that's his problem if he doesn't want to. So, she will join the Guard and make a difference. With their help, she will destroy Pharma Corp and Orion.

Finally, they arrived at their destination. Mateo and Ivan were comfortably chatting, and Onyx followed quietly behind them. The building was higher than she had anticipated. She expected Florida to be more suburban. Instead, this city has strange, oval-shaped skyscrapers and no drones flying around.

She had never left the tristate area other than for overseas deployments, and with those, she didn't get to experience the cities she visited.

Ivan held the door open, and Onyx thanked him as she walked through. *See, I have manners*, she thought and smiled. Mateo constantly nagged that she needed to work on her people skills.

"You're in a good mood," Mateo muttered.

"Oh, baby, just looking at you turns me on, making me happy," she said in a loud whisper and giggled. She was teasing. She knew he was irritated with her, so why not have fun with it?

He looked at her perplexed. Onyx wasn't usually this playful, and he didn't know how to answer, so he was glad that Ivan had finished signing them in and was ready to escort them up.

The building had many large windows and a massive desk with armed uniform personnel. In addition, escalators and a row of elevators stood nearby.

They took one of the elevators up to the top floor. The fluorescent lights were so bright that they hurt Onyx's eyes. Then they entered a large office.

"Sir!" Ivan said, saluting a large man behind the desk.

"As you were," he said coolly and extended his hand to Mateo.

What happened to ladies first? I hope he's not like that in bed, she thought, noticing his attractiveness. But unfortunately, he was wearing his uniform too, not that a man in uniform wasn't sexy, only that it seemed unnecessary.

"Mateo Martinez. Thank you for having us," Mateo said.

Onyx also shook his hand. "Onyx Pion. We are grateful to be here," she told him with a warm smile.

"General Jones, at your service," he said to both. "Please, sit." Then, he motioned toward the two empty chairs across from his desk.

Ivan excused himself and left the office.

"I want to begin by commending you both on your bravery. Escaping tyranny is no small feat. I hope your stay has been pleasant," he said.

"It has, and we are forever in your debt," Onyx replied before Mateo could.

Mateo wasn't thrilled by her choice of words. He didn't want to owe anyone anything. Still, he knew she had deliberately answered that way, hoping Mateo would feel obligated to accept whatever position the general offered.

What is this game she's playing? Not only does she turn my life upside down, but now, she wants to manipulate me into something I don't want to do, he thought.

"I understand you have some compromising information, young lady, that you risked your life to obtain and get it here. I'd like to hear all about it, and just so you're reassured, this is with no commitment. We are a free nation. We do not force or coerce anyone into service. We only want volunteers of their own free will and for their love of this country committed to our security and defense. However, we'd like to know if there is anything we can use to better defend and maintain our sovereignty. All is fair in love and war," he said.

"It's a lot of information, but I'll summarize as best I can. And I'll admit that much of it is very scientific. So I can understand its basic concept, but I'll advise you to get your lead scientists to review it."

He looked at her with interest, and Mateo wished he could excuse himself and find Ivan. He came here to be free of the military complex machine, and here he is, hauled into something they literally cannot change (or dragged into something that will make no difference as Onyx hoped that the Guard would go to war, and Mateo knew that was not likely). She doesn't realize or accept that people in New York were willing participants. They get everything they are experiencing for "safety's sake" and are ready to surrender every human right to feel secure.

"The pandemic of 2019 was not real," she began. "It was engineered in a lab, deliberately."

Mateo rolled his eyes as she spoke. *Here we go*, he thought.

"This was planned to introduce the vaccines, which had no virus. Instead, they were transgenic substances with the pretense of preventing the virus. They have ribonucleic acid and deoxyribonucleic acid," she continued.

A self-taught scientist vigilante, Mateo thought, containing laughter.

"Most importantly, they are ribonucleic acid messengers," she continued, encouraged by the general's apparent curiosity. He was hanging on every word she said, and the more she spoke, the crazier it sounded to Mateo.

"Viruses and these ribonucleic acids are messengers, codes; letters that go and inform our bodies to create a substance, ribosome. So what we call a vaccine is the introduction of ribonucleic acid which will cause our ribosome to create a protein like a said virus. These vaccines use a similar coded method as the ribonucleic acid, go to the nucleus, and modify the most intimate aspect of our being … our personality, which is coded entirely in our genome, in every cell in our bodies," she carried on, and Mateo cringed.

"That was the intended target—to enter the body using the adenovirus to change the personality. Still, it's bigger than that. It involves nanotechnology that targets specific types of cells in the body. One can easily inhale nanotech, and the delivery method is a chemtrail, sprayed from ten thousand to twenty thousand feet to avoid commercial air traffic and better control the diffusion into a local area. They used marker planes to lay down indicators marking the borders for heavier planes to spray metric tons of nanotech particulates into the region below," Onyx said passionately.

The general was enthralled, and she continued. "Their advances in functional nucleic acids and DNA nanotechnology have made it possible to use DNA as a new and promising molecular tool kit for controlling receptor-mediated signaling and cell fates. They can literally control anyone on the planet with this tech and even kill. Remember when people voluntarily gave their DNA to know their ancestry?" she asked, and he nodded.

"Well, we served the most intimate aspect of our humanity on a silver platter—biowarfare using DNA to design viruses targeting specific individuals. So, General, if you ever gave up your DNA, know that you're not safe," she said, and he sat up straight.

I'll admit, she's a good storyteller, Mateo thought, concealing a laugh with a cough.

She continued, explaining how people are under a spell, an illusion. It resulted in younger generations developing chronic diseases, dying prematurely, and becoming increasingly dependent on prescribed pharmaceuticals since the pandemic's vaccination mandates began.

She also went into the surveillance of citizens, how many were vocal against the government, imprisoned as threats to national security, and accused of terrorism. Finally, she mentioned how pharmaceutical companies have power equivalent to that of the governments and how technocrats run the show.

She went on, and Mateo wanted it to end. Onyx suppressed all these feelings out of fear and was now free to express herself with liberty.

Tell him how you "really" feel, Onyx, Mateo thought.

She had never expressed any of this loathing to him, probably because he had not seen her in four years. Mateo didn't like how things were going over there, so he decided to leave, but he did not intend to put on a cape and save the world. No one was coming to rescue them. We can only be the change we wish to see and save ourselves.

"They don't have to force vaccines on the population anymore. They have privatized the farmlands and introduced this technology into our food supply. Any government who lies, deceives, and does not have the best interest of its citizens as a priority deserves and should be overthrown," she concluded.

Mateo felt a chill race down his spine. Those were dangerous words to utter to a general in the armed forces of any nation, but that was Onyx: fearless to a fault. What she failed to comprehend was that those citizens were complicit.

The phone on his desk rang. He answered it and only said, "Roger," then hung up.

Onyx handed him a flash drive. They shook hands, and then the general excused himself. "I look forward to meeting with you both again very soon. It was my pleasure," he said and hurried out of the office.

Shortly after he had left, Ivan returned. "Hey, guys, pardon his leaving so abruptly. There was an urgent matter he must attend to. We will schedule another visit sometime in the future. How about we grab something to eat, and I show you both around town?" he asked.

"Sounds great," Mateo said, eager to leave.

They went to a nearby restaurant. "This is downtown Miami," Ivan informed them as they sat. The place was full of people.

There weren't many restaurants back home, and those still open were often empty. Only the elite enjoyed those things now. Also, the population in New York City had significantly decreased.

Mateo and Ivan did most of the talking. Onyx was glad just to eat. She ordered fried calamari as an appetizer, a sex-on-the-beach cocktail, and grilled salmon with mashed potatoes and vegetables as her entrée.

Mateo and Ivan both drank beer and ate steak. After their meal, they all had coffee. Then Onyx wanted to hurry back to the hotel room to have Mateo for dessert.

That night in the hotel room, Mateo was oddly quiet. Onyx knew she had gotten under his skin, but she didn't expect him to give her the silent treatment.

"You OK?" she asked.

"I'm good," he said sharply, heading toward the door. "Going out for a run," he said, shutting it behind him.

Onyx was annoyed he left without her having her dessert.

Mateo wasn't in the mood to discuss why he was upset yet. Her antics were utterly disrespectful and uncalled for. He respected her desire to join the Guard, although he disagreed with her underlying motives. However, he honored her wishes.

On the contrary, Onyx had no boundaries regarding his need to do something different. Therefore, assuming she knew best what he should do was the highest form of disregard for his feelings.

Only we know what is best for us, what rings true in our hearts. No one can dictate what we should do or how we should do it. Not a single soul will take our place at death, so not a single one should direct the course of our lives.

He ran faster than he wanted, his mind racing with thoughts and emotions, but he was still upset. It wasn't comfortable to run with that much humidity. He would have to get used to this type of climate. Everything in life is about flexibility. In any environment, the resilient species thrives and survives. Change is constant, and the ability to adapt separates the weak from the strong.

After running a few miles, Mateo walked, unsure how many more miles he had covered. Still, it felt like he'd been walking forever. *Sometimes what we want isn't what we need, and we expend so much energy desiring things incompatible with our highest and best good,* he thought.

"*We further exhaust ourselves, attempting to change people so that they can fit into the narrative of what we want,*" he muttered, seemingly trying to convince himself.

Unfortunately, he and Onyx were not on the same page, and it seemed they'd have to go their separate ways.

"What is meant to be always finds its way," he said to himself, returning to the hotel.

PART SEVEN

In the morning, Onyx and Mateo went out for breakfast. She looks extra good in tight jeans, a tank top with no bra, and even wearing red lipstick, making what Mateo was about to do even more difficult.

As they ate, Mateo told her what he had decided.

"Tomorrow, I'm leaving for that community off the grid I was talking about, and you're welcome to come. I know you've set your mind on joining the Guard, and if that's what you want, best of luck with that," he said and continued to eat, not looking at her.

What the fuck is this? He's too sensitive, she thought. "Whatever. If that's what you want to do, I'm not going to stop you," she said.

Onyx was furious, though. He was earnest about moving with that cult to the middle of nowhere. *I guess I don't mean shit to him,* she thought.

Mateo didn't reply. He came here with a plan and was glad he was able to help Onyx get out. But aside from that, he wasn't going to join the Guard for her sake.

Mateo never told Onyx he was coming here, intending to continue in a military career. Instead, he had explicitly expressed his plan to move to Eden. If she had made other plans for them, that was her issue to sort out. It was she who had planned to leave without him. Where? he never asked, but she would be dead if it were not for him.

He didn't understand how she had made this decision so rashly. Onyx had not been here a day when she decided she would join their Guard to change the world. Her childhood traumas were responsible for her decisions, and the need to belong was apparent. But unfortunately, this wasn't a subject Mateo could address.

Onyx shut herself off and pretended everything was perfect, that she was perfect. Mateo can't help her if she doesn't see a problem.

But what one perceives as a problem can be something one wants to change, and a person will only change if that's what they want to do.

"It is what I want to do and precisely what I told you I had planned before coming here. So I don't know why you'd think I would do anything different," Mateo said after a while, looking at her, hoping she would answer without being condescending.

She looked up to meet his gaze. "I just thought that after everything we went through, you would be angry and want to get back at the pieces of shit trying to kill us," she said, disappointed.

He sighed. "I have no intention of retaliating. How could I? It's irrational to think that we can take on Orion. What makes you think these people here will support you in those endeavors anyway?" he asked.

She doesn't know anything. She's making decisions based on assumptions, hopes, and dreams, Mateo thought as he drank his coffee.

The garden omelet he was eating was mediocre at best … undercooked and missing ingredients. So he ordered some pancakes to compensate.

"I don't care about anything left behind," he continued. "I'm glad I made it out alive, and I want to put that behind me. If you want to go after them and think this government will support you, more power to you, but this is where we part ways. I will not be involved with any of that shit anymore," he said, taking a plate of waffles.

He looked at the plate. It wasn't pancakes, but he had no energy to address it because he had enough with Onyx. He only hoped they were good.

She took a drink from her cup of unsweetened black coffee. "I understand and thank you for helping me get here. But we both need to do what we feel is right," she told him indifferently.

She was trying to guilt him into doing what was "right"!

Right for whom? We, the people, never win. She's delusional, he thought.

He didn't reply, and they finished eating in silence. That night at the hotel room, Mateo packed whatever belongings he had and made calls to ensure all arrangements were still on schedule for his trip to Eden. Once he finished packing, he went to take a shower. He and Onyx still had not said another word to each other.

Onyx was watching something on the television. She didn't want to admit it, but she didn't want him to leave. However, he had made up his mind, and nothing was left for her to say. She never discussed her feelings, and she wasn't going to start now. Onyx was unsure what she felt, and if she did admit that she loved Mateo or something of that nature, would he stay?

Of course, there would only be one way to find out.

Mateo returned from showering wearing only boxers and lay beside her on the bed, hoping to get some rest, but Onyx had other plans.

She slid her hand into his boxers and kissed his neck. "Might as well get a proper goodbye," she said, nibbling his earlobe.

If he was determined to leave, the sex was what she would miss the most, so she would make the best of tonight just in case it was their last chance for intimacy.

The next day, Mateo rose early and went for a run. Onyx was still sleeping when he returned, and he was glad. He took a shower and dressed quietly. Then he went to the nightstand and wrote Onyx a note. He took his bag, and taking one last glance back, he whispered, "Good luck," and shut the door.

Later, Onyx stretched and opened her eyes, feeling rested. Looking around, she noticed Mateo wasn't in bed.

She got up and went to the bathroom. He wasn't there either. His bag was gone. "Wow, he left without saying goodbye!" she exclaimed aloud.

Mateo didn't need to help her, yet he did. Maybe she had behaved ungratefully, and now he was gone. It hurt. He was the only family, friend—anything she had—and she managed to push him away.

Oh well, maybe it's for the best. Mateo would only be a distraction, she thought, getting in the shower.

Days seemed to last forever. It was Friday, and they had a meeting with the general on Monday. Ivan was supposed to send a car for them.

She wondered if Mateo had told Ivan that he was leaving or had just left without mentioning anything to him. "I guess I'll find out on Monday," she mumbled.

Looking around the room, she saw the note on the nightstand. *"Onyx, I hope you find what you need here, and I hope you find happiness. Know I'll always be there for you. Good luck, Mateo."*

She read it over and over. *That's all?* she thought. The jerk could've said more. *Why go after me? Why not let me run alone if he would give up eventually?* "Fucking coward," she whispered.

Onyx expected a declaration of love, but how can one expect that which they cannot give?

She sat on the bed, overcome by sadness, still holding the note. She looked at the window, the sun shining through, bright and happy, yet she felt sad. *Why didn't I go with him?* she wondered.

What did she want? What would make her happy? Although she didn't have the answers to those questions, Onyx would do what she did best.

First, she will join the Guard. After that, she will use their resources to find and kill Kyle. Finally, if she can't destroy Orion and Pharma Corp, she will at least have her revenge.

Most of the weekend she spent in the room reminiscing about simpler times, when she was young and innocent, the days she met Mateo and wanted nothing more than to get away by joining the military.

She hated school, the fucking kids all trying to be cool and fit in. She made no friends, not one—ever.

After a while, she was glad to switch schools constantly. There would always be those other lonely rejects who would spot her a mile away and think they could be friends. Onyx despised those kids the most. She didn't want any friends. She wanted out.

Onyx recalled walking into the recruiting office, so nervous she felt faint, the taste of vomit in her mouth. It's fascinating how people evolve with time and often radically change. She was seventeen years old, unsure, timid, and naïve.

Now, she is everything but that.

Mateo walked up to her immediately and greeted her with enthusiasm. He seemed confident. He was young and handsome, with a bright and charming smile.

"Hello, there," he had said, extending his hand to her. "Mateo Martinez," he introduced himself. "What can I do for you?" he asked eagerly.

"M&M," she said without thought, and he laughed.

"Yes, those are my initials. What's your name?" he asked, looking at her, intrigued.

"Onyx Pion," she replied slowly.

He raised an eyebrow. "How can I help you?" he said, hoping this time she would say why she was there; she did not seem like the type to enlist.

"I want to enlist," she said matter-of-factly.

"Do you, now?" he asked, smiling. "Well, I'm your guy," he said before she could reply.

"What? You don't think I can do it?" she asked, obviously insulted.

"I believe you can do anything you set your mind to; I was only being funny. Why else would you be here?" he lied.

His job was not to make those judgments but to recruit, and basic training would weed out those who did not belong. However, he did make a mental note that she was sensitive and combative. The latter would help her in the military, but she had to toughen that skin if she was going to survive.

Onyx was in bed, tossing and turning. The television was on, but she had not been watching it. Instead, her mind was racing, flooded by thoughts of the past. It was uncharacteristic of her to dwell on the past because she liked to pretend it never existed, but she attempted to remember old times with Mateo. Obviously, instead of helping, it gave her anxiety.

Onyx was self-centered and egotistical. She only thought of herself. She justified it by reasoning that she never had anyone to depend on but herself, which is why she prioritized her interest over others. Although not entirely misplaced, she was merely surviving and attempting to minimize disappointment.

Mateo Martinez was selfless, kind, and thoughtful. *M&M*, she thought with a smile. "God, it's been ages since I've called him that," she said to the ceiling.

Now she was talking to herself. The last time she called Mateo M&M was when she left for basic training. Upon return, Onyx was different, distant, and less dependent. Even more reticent than she had been, she never called him that again.

Onyx drifted away from Mateo, and once she began working for Orion, she stopped talking to him for extended periods. He resented her for it, and after many failed attempts to catch up, he stopped trying.

Pondering all they had gone through in the decade or so they'd known each other, she was surprised that he had even considered helping her as he did in the first place. His friendship was unconditional. He was always there for Onyx, no matter what. And unfortunately, people like that are hard to come by.

"I don't deserve any of what he has done for me," she said, opening the small refrigerator and grabbing a beer.

She took a long drink from the bottle. It was cold and refreshing. She sat on the bed again and continued to recall her memories with Mateo.

While hiking with him, she slipped, and he caught her before she hit the ground. That was the first time she felt physically attracted to him. His touch exhilarated her, and her heart began to race. She had never been this close with anyone before. While in foster care, there were always other children, but none she connected with. All the kids she ended up with were mean and mostly fought.

After that hiking incident, she unconsciously started flirting with Mateo. Then while at the library on another occasion a few months later, he pulled her into an open closet and kissed her. She was so excited and aroused by his spontaneity that she went into a frenzy and undressed him. She wanted him inside her badly. That was her first sexual experience.

Onyx knew he did not intend for it to go that far, but she could not help herself. She was not the romantic type, but that was one of her fondest memories.

She wondered what he was doing. She longed for him. She was used to being alone, but she had grown accustomed to him during the past couple of weeks they were together.

"I guess you don't know what you have till it's gone!" she exclaimed, drinking the last of her beer. Mateo was the best thing in her life, the one constant. Since she first met him, he had always been there for her, and just thinking about him being out of her life for good was upsetting.

Most of her best memories were with Mateo, and what little happiness she's ever felt was associated with him. Onyx's happiest memory without Mateo was turning eighteen on April tenth. Although it was an uneventful day in Witch Perez's house, it was the best day of her life.

It's hard to believe it was ten ago. Onyx skipped graduation. The George Washington HS Class of 2020 sucked, if you asked her.

The television was still on, so she shut it off. Perhaps if she slept early, she could make this dragging weekend go faster. But Monday could not come soon enough. She needed something to do. She had to keep busy.

Onyx was anxious to join the Guard and get to work. She disliked being idle. The mind was our worst enemy, and the best way to subdue it was to keep busy. But unfortunately, sleep did not come easy. Finally, frustrated, she covered her face with the pillow and screamed, "Damn it, Mateo; screw you!"

She sat up. *Where exactly is that fucking place anyway?* she thought. "Who cares? He decided to leave, so that's it. I'll never look for him again. That's the last he will ever see of me!" she shouted.

Talking to herself always helped calm her down, but she had difficulty understanding her emotions. Did she love Mateo? That is not something she ever considered or thought about in the past.

Love wasn't part of her vocabulary. She either liked people or didn't, and by "liking," she meant to tolerate.

Mateo was her friend. They were intimate, and she liked him, but these feelings were unfamiliar. Missing people was not part of her range of emotions either. For her, people served a purpose in your life; upon completion, they leave, and you should not get attached. However, she missed Mateo and did not know how to reconcile these feelings.

Who knows if she would ever see Mateo again. She didn't even know where he was. But she knew he had disappeared in the swamps and left, like the coward he was, without saying goodbye.

The best thing to do now was to forget him and stay busy. They chose different paths. Mateo had achieved his purpose in her life. It was time to move on and find people more aligned with who she was.

PART EIGHT

The drive to Eden was long, and although Mateo had dozed on and off for most of the ride, he felt tired, maybe because the nymphomaniac didn't let him sleep, and he woke at sunrise. He felt terrible for not saying goodbye and knew she would be upset. He only hoped she saw the note.

He knew that he loved Onyx and was sure that he would miss her. The truth was that Mateo already did, but he also recognized that she was full of uncertainty, and he deserved better. There was nothing he would not do for her. He would be there if she ever needed him, but he would not allow her to rope him into a physical relationship with no emotional payoff. It was draining. The sex was good. Hell, *phenomenal*, but Mateo wanted more, and she was unavailable.

Life is about identifying harmful things to our general well-being before they become destructive or before we develop resentment. It was a difficult task because it involved letting go.

Had he allowed himself to stay and done things he honestly did not want to do, all because he was in love and was willing to please her by putting her needs before his own, he would end up unhappy and possibly hating her.

There is a thin line between love and hate, and it never has to do with the other person, but with our unwillingness to accept that the person is not suitable for us and the delusion that, somehow, we will change them.

There were only two simple choices: accept people as they are or recognize they are incompatible with us. Of course, it is easier said than done, but we need to have the strength and resolve to always do the best things for ourselves, even if they hurt initially.

Mateo was confident that he had made the right choice and was looking forward to seeing friends he had not seen in a long time. But suddenly, he felt a pang of grief. Onyx had no one. He tried for so long to grasp what that was like, and the more he did, the more he understood Onyx. Knowing a person was not always possible without understanding them.

We know people and often become judgmental of them when we dislike certain behaviors, and there were many things he disliked about Onyx. Still, he understood her, which allowed him to be empathetic.

He could distinguish the reasons that drove her to behave the way she did. He felt a need to help, to save her from herself, but she would not allow it. But on the other hand, she may not see any issues and wasn't a damsel in distress.

Onyx was fully aware of who she was and what she wanted, and he had no right to infringe upon her will. And having come to that conclusion, leaving was the best decision for both of them. He could see how they would both become resentful in a relationship. The signs were there, so having the courage to walk away would save them endless heartache.

Good thing he walked away before it even got started. How many people ignore the early red flags, only to regret it later?

He got off the bus with a few other people and looked around.

"Mateo!" Cynthia ran over and embraced him. "I knew you would come eventually," she said, smiling with her infectious and magnetic energy.

Cynthia was one of those people that radiated positivity and exuded light. She made those around her feel good. It's addictive to be in her presence because her energy is powerfully contagious. People like her were unforgettable, and encountering them was a privilege.

The air was moist here. Mateo heard flies buzzing in his ear, and his clothes were already sticking to his body. His boots were heavy with mud. *This should be fun*, he thought.

"So good to see you, Cyn. I've missed you," he said, following her.

They reached an open space of somewhat dry land with a log cabin. Mateo followed Cynthia in.

"You must be exhausted. I have some food ready for you." Cynthia pointed at a small table in the middle of the cottage.

"Freshen up and take a nap. You'll be undisturbed. We'll catch up later," she said. Her ability to read a person was unmatched, and her maternal instinct was part of her charm.

"Thank you," Mateo said, and she smiled.

She excused herself and closed the cabin door. While Mateo was thrilled to be there and see her, he was glad to be alone. Some food and a nap would be helpful.

He looked around but didn't see a bathroom. Only a bucket of water was by the door, and he wondered if that was what she meant by "freshening up."

Mateo woke up disoriented, as if he should be elsewhere. *I guess that was a good nap*, he thought. But unfortunately, he was drenched in sweat. There was no air-conditioning, and it was hot and humid.

Civilized living has its perks. Mateo chuckled at the thought.

He could almost hear Onyx complaining about how it was "hot as hell" and saying something like, "You wanted to be off the grid, and now, the mosquitos own your ass." He loved her dark sense of humor.

The mosquitos *were* relentless. Mateo was also experiencing a whole new set of sounds. He heard dripping water, croaking frogs, buzzing flies, and other strange animal noises. There was also an eerie silence, although he did hear chatter in the distance.

By now, he had a pretty good number of mosquito bites on his legs. Walking out of the cabin, he saw a young man sitting on a chair. The cottage had two beds and a small table with a chair. He supposed the one he was sitting on was part of the set.

Mateo walked up to him and said, "Hey, man, I'm Mateo."

The young man stood up and took his extended hand. "Yeah, Cynthia has told me all about you. I'll be your cabin mate. You can call me Carlito."

Carlito wore cargo denim shorts and a black tank with army boots.

They shook hands, and Carlito put the chair back inside the cabin. "I'll show you around," he said as he stepped back outside toward Mateo, who was looking around in amazement.

There were other larger cabins in the distance, which looked like a mess hall. Farther away stood a row of latrine huts.

"Wow, from what I remember, this lot of land used to be empty. Not a single structure was here when they purchased it. So although it's come a long way, I feel guilty that I come now after all the work is done, without contributing to the building efforts," Mateo said, wondering if he would be able to adapt.

Carlito turned to face him. "Man, the work here is *never* done. There is *always* something to do, something to farm, something to repair, and something to build. You will earn your keep, that I promise," he said, and they laughed and continued walking.

"I guess freedom comes with hard work, so people quickly surrender it for comfort," Mateo said, following him along the trail.

"Yeah, that's why Cypher said, 'ignorance is bliss' in *The Matrix* and wanted to plug back in," Carlito said.

"Would you go back?" Mateo asked, not sure if he regretted being out there.

"Never. I'd rather die on my feet than live on my knees," he said, turning to face Mateo, who followed behind him.

"I hear that. Hey, man, were you in the service on the other side?" Mateo asked.

"Sure was. I am willing to die for what I believe in; unfortunately, I lost hope, but I believe in this here, and I'll die defending it," Carlito said as he walked on.

Mateo admired people with conviction and valued Onyx's tenacity regardless of disagreements.

Finally, it was Monday. Onyx woke up early, went for a run, had breakfast, and was ready long before the car arrived.

A receptionist at the front desk called, informing her that her ride was there waiting outside, so she rushed down, taking the stairs.

The same gentleman driving the last time was in the driver's seat, but Ivan had not come to fetch her, and she was relieved. She was not interested in small talk with him. She couldn't tolerate him. She felt he was a needy people pleaser and major ass kisser. He reminded her of the kids in school who would try to make her acquaintance, unaware she had no desire to fit in, be liked, or make friends.

The young soldier driving didn't say much. "What's the Guard like?" Onyx asked him.

"It's great," he said, looking at her through the mirror.

"We're you born on this side?" she asked.

"Yes, ma'am," he said proudly.

"Lucky you," she said, and they rode the rest of the trip in silence.

Once she arrived at the building in downtown Miami, Ivan greeted her. "Good morning," he said, ushering her into the building. "I received a message from Mateo. Unfortunately, I understand he will not be joining us. Pity. I know him, and he's a good man; would've been a great asset to us," he said.

He finished signing her in, and they proceeded to the elevators, "As long as he's happy, that's all that matters," she said while they waited.

He looked at her questioningly. "Are you two together?" he asked hesitantly.

Ivan could sense that she wasn't fond of him and was unsure what kind of reply she would give him, but his curiosity got the best of him. He was hoping Mateo would join their ranks, and he could ask him about Onyx, but that wasn't going to happen.

"Mateo and I have known each other a long time. I can't say we are together without mentioning it is somewhat complicated. However, that is all past tense now. Whatever we had … or didn't, for that matter … is over. I will be forever grateful. He has done more for me than anyone else my entire life, but it's time to move on without him." She said more than she wanted to say.

It was unlike Onyx to volunteer so much information in one breath, but apparently, she was more wounded about Mateo's sudden departure than she was willing to admit.

"I've known Mateo even longer. He's a great guy and any woman's loss," Ivan said, taking a shot at Onyx. He was looking for a yes or no response, but since she was in a venting mood, he seized the opportunity to remind her how great Mateo was.

Onyx would've given him a one-word answer any other time, but she was struggling without Mateo. She felt like a usurper. It was him they wanted. How could they trust her under the circumstances she arrived here?

"I'm better than Mateo any day of the week and twice on Sunday, I promise you that, buddy," she said to Ivan, bruised by his comment.

Selfish! she told herself. *You don't give a shit about Mateo. He is only a means to an end. You needed him here to attest on your behalf, to reassure them that you are trustworthy; that they need you. It's all about you,* she thought.

"Of course, it's all about me. If I don't look out for us, who will?" Onyx told herself, shaking her head.

They entered the general's office. "Welcome back," he said, beaming.

He was a fine-looking man, not as old as one would expect him to be in that rank. He couldn't be more than ten years her senior. He was tall and muscular, a big man. Returning the smile, she wondered if everything else was big.

"It's good to be here, sir," she said, shaking his hand while squeezing extra tight.

"I'm glad to hear that," Jones said as he sat. His desk was massive. A photograph of a beautiful redhead stood on it, and the wall behind him was a showcase of certificates and accolades.

"I must say, there was a lot of information in that file you gave me. But, unfortunately, you didn't mention the half of it," he said, reclining in his chair.

"I tried to tell you what was most significant," she said, playing with her hair.

"There is so much I want to discuss with you. Firstly, we'd like to have you as a private consultant. The pay will be good, and we will cover housing, expenses, and a vehicle. Second, I suggest you acquire a weapon as soon as possible. Ivan can assist you with that. First, however, you need to register it into our database," he said to her, cutting to the chase.

Her excitement was evident. "When do I start?" she exclaimed, raising her hands.

"I have your contract right here. Go over it and sign it," said General Jones, handing her the papers.

Onyx took the papers and read through them carefully. Ivan was standing behind her, anxiously waiting for her to finish and wishing Mateo was also there.

Onyx flipped the pages as she continued to read. She felt a little sad that she was doing this without Mateo. Onyx felt she was usurping his spot, but then she realized he had made his choice with utter disregard for her feelings and was entirely ungrateful to General Jones.

Honestly, she didn't care what the contract said. She just wanted to get started. Onyx started working early, and doing nothing drove her crazy. Without work or Mateo, she had an excess of energy and no means of channeling it.

"Looks good to me," she finally said, signing the contract.

"Welcome aboard. I look forward to working with you," General Jones stated, shaking her hand once more.

"Congratulations. I promise you'll love it here," Ivan assured her.

Onyx beamed excitedly, looking forward to this new chapter in her life. She hoped to spring roots and call this place home.

Carlito showed Mateo the entire complex. Everything and everyone served a purpose. The organization and functionality of things were commendable, and Mateo was impressed. He was happy that everything seemed to run smoothly.

"I see you've met your roommate," Cynthia said, joining them at a lunch table.

"Yes, I have. Carlito has been helpful and informative," Mateo said.

"Good," she said, smiling.

"Hey, Carlito, come play with us, man," another young man called out.

"See you later, guys. They need their star player," Carlito said, and he ran off. A soccer game was about to start, and they needed a warm body.

Carlito had asked Mateo if he played soccer as he showed him around. Mateo told him he wasn't very good at it, but he was willing to get better.

"No better way to keep fit and entertained than sports," Carlito told him.

Mateo was staring at some trees that appeared to be growing upside down. *This is a strange place*, he thought distractedly.

"How are you?" Cynthia asked once they were alone, bringing Mateo back from contemplation. She looked at him, concerned. Cynthia had run a foundation for veterans and developed the idea for this place. Mateo frequently attended meetings at the center and volunteered there.

He liked what she was doing for the homeless guys who suffered from alcohol and drug addiction. New Hope was a haven for them when all else was lost, primarily thanks to Cynthia.

Cynthia was a free spirit, caring and generous. However, he never imagined that she would accomplish this. All her ideas sounded good in theory, but he felt they were farfetched; yet, here they were.

It was no surprise she pulled this off, though. She was persuasive, and her zest for life was worthy of admiration. People would follow her to the ends of the earth. All it took to accomplish anything was to believe you could. Cynthia was never discouraged by the naysayers. She felt that she could, and she did. She wasn't that different from Onyx. Believing in oneself was the key to success. Maybe it seemed crazy to Mateo what Onyx was trying to do, just like it did when Cynthia proposed this idea to him years ago. Yet, here he was in the manifestation of what Cynthia knew, without a doubt, would eventually come to pass.

Mateo was very close with Cynthia's brother, Nathan, whom he had not yet seen. Nathan helped Cynthia run that foundation back home, and even though she and Mateo maintained more of a professional acquaintance, they seemed to have connected.

"I'm good," he said, and she stared at him disbelievingly.

Mateo didn't want to admit it, but the last couple of weeks had been a lot for him. It's like he's in one of those weird dreams where you're in one place, and the next minute, you're in another … only that a lifetime happens in between.

"If you say so," she smiled, and he couldn't help but smile. She was like a sun, radiant.

"Where's Nathan?" Mateo asked, looking around. There were more people here than he expected, all friendly and with a happy disposition.

Energy must be contagious. Everyone is miserable back home, and even if you try to cheer up once you come around large groups of people, you cannot help but feel down. Here, it's the opposite. Even if you're down, you feel good, he thought as he saw an insect he could not name.

"He's probably in the kitchen or on a water run. Things don't come easy here, but I promise, it's worth it," she said, laughing as though he was in for more than he bargained.

"Nothing good ever comes easy," he said, shaking his head and laughing. She made him feel better already.

Mateo was still thinking about Onyx and trying to settle in. Coming here was a drastic change because he didn't like significant changes. He had a stable life. He grew up in the neighborhood he still lived in and with most of his friends he had known since childhood, so this relocation was terrifying.

Mateo and Cynthia talked for a while. She continued to explain the operations of this sanctuary, and they discussed what work would best suit him when suddenly, someone hugged him from behind.

"There he is," Nathan said, now ruffling his hair. Nathan was a slim guy, but he was strong. He shaved his head and had flawless dark skin like his sister. In addition, he had kind brown eyes and was super funny.

Mateo got up, and they hugged. "Good to see you, Nate. How have you been?" he asked warmly.

Nathan was smiling brightly. He and Cynthia had that in common; they were joyful and charismatic.

"Better now that you're here, my friend. Come on, let me show you some cool shit," he said to Mateo.

They took off, and Mateo waved back at Cynthia, who was jubilantly watching them. Happiness consists of finding your tribe, the people that make your heart sing and surrendering to its unfolding.

This community did not only consist of soldiers. Cynthia also managed to convince people of all backgrounds who were miserable with their current situation and life to leave and settle here. For her, it was easy since she was a holistic counselor with a wide range of patients.

Teachers, farmers, nurses, doctors, scientists, construction workers, musicians, and many more positively contributed to this new, self-sustaining society. Mateo was apprehensive about leaving, but the whole incident with Onyx was the deciding factor, and he was glad he made a choice.

This peace is the kind Mateo craved and needed.

Onyx wanted to keep him in her chaos. She was addicted to the thrill. She created her storms and then complained because it rained. She was always looking for something to fill her void, unable to sit still with herself.

Mateo only hoped she didn't bring Ivan and the Guard pandemonium.

PART NINE

Mateo was happy to be at Eden. He had been considering coming here for a long time, and ironically, he had told Nathan and Cynthia that he was coming only a week before Onyx came back into his life.

It was serendipitous that fate would reunite them before he was gone, and Onyx could never find him again. He thought her return was a sign that she would join him here, and they'd live happily ever after. But sadly, he was wrong. So often, it is the expectations that break a heart and not the individual.

I served my purpose in Onyx's life. I hope she's happy with the choice she made, Mateo thought as he assisted Nathan with repairing a cabin.

Every day there was work to do as Carlito promised, and Mateo kept busy. Cynthia was right; nothing at Eden came easy, but Mateo was happy to be there. Mateo had no qualms about working for his freedom and livelihood. However, peace and the sovereignty to choose are what he valued most.

Things were different postpandemic and war. Russia had not won, but neither did the West. They failed to prevent Russia from occupying many already vulnerable nations, and the allied influence had weakened.

There was palpable tension. People distrusted the government, which led to further surveillance, and if you were labeled a domestic terrorist, officials would seize your bank accounts. If you were in opposition, they would jail you, and many allegedly committed "suicide" at an alarming number.

There was no free speech. Fact-checkers were now digital thugs working for the government or corporations to maintain their interests. They silenced anyone who challenged the prescribed narrative, removing them from all digital existence, which meant everyday life since nothing existed outside the Metaverse and the internet.

People were ostracized and labeled antisomething. Naturally, many fled. I suppose that's why Onyx so ardently wanted to fight—a worthy desire, yet one that would bear no good fruits.

People were always free to choose, accepting the dystopia they now experienced. Nothing was absolute. No one had the power to rule another without permission.

People were not aware of the power they possessed. It all ended when they decided to reject a system that had failed them and create something new.

Although the many can defeat the few if they choose to, that is easier said than done because people have no concept of freedom. Instead, they believe they must obey, ensuring their comfort and safety. Most people are unwilling to build a civilization from scratch, and if humanity depended on it, they'd become extinct.

Mateo wasn't a pessimist but had little hope for humanity. An old saying states that the greatest trick the devil ever played was convincing people he didn't exist. That, in some symbolic way, was true. To convince people they had no power and no capacity to decide what was best for them was a genius trick governments have played since the inception of time.

"To each his own, as long as we respect individual choices and do not infringe on the liberties and safety of others. Let everyone live as they wish," Mateo told Carlito before falling asleep.

Onyx had settled into her new life in the past six months. She felt that she had finally found where she belonged.

She was still helping decipher the information from the laptop with the intelligence team and had been able to tolerate Ivan somewhat. He was a nice guy, and she could see why he and Mateo were friends.

What Onyx wanted, though, was to be sent back on a recon mission. This desire was to satisfy her need for revenge. She still hadn't gotten over how Kyle tried to kill her, but General Jones opposed the idea of sending Onyx back.

She needed the Guard's help and resources. Without it, going back to kill Kyle would prove impossible.

Last week, they went out for drinks. Onyx insisted that General Jones should join them and after everyone had gone and she was alone with the general, she kissed him.

"I've wanted to do that since I signed that contract, but I saw your wedding ring. I know you're still grieving your wife's passing, but you deserve to be happy," she said as he looked at her, surprised.

She kissed him again, and finding no resistance, she took his hand and led him out. Outside, he seized her before she got in the car and passionately kissed her, moving his hands up her skirt.

She pressed hard against him, feeling his erection, and got excited.

"Is it wrong to seduce a grieving widower?" she asked herself, getting into his car. However, she did find him irresistibly attractive; he *was* a sexy man.

Onyx needed to relieve some tension. It had been awhile, and Mateo was a distant memory. He left without saying goodbye and hadn't reached out to her once. Onyx wouldn't admit it, but she resented him for it.

She expected to hear from Mateo the first few weeks, even if only to ask how she was doing … but nothing. She asked Ivan a few times if he had heard from Mateo, and Ivan said no.

What a piece of shit, she thought the last time she asked Ivan. *The least he can do is stay in touch with the friend who helped us get here*, she thought bitterly.

After a while, though, she decided thinking about Mateo was a waste of time and set her sights on General Jones.

It started as a silly crush, but as she got to know him, it turned into admiration and then evolved into her liking him and wanting to spend time with him alone after the passing of his wife.

Onyx and Jones hooked up as if they had just gotten out of prison; it was intense, and they did it again in the morning. Onyx thought Jones was her perfect match, and their ideals aligned. They were both ambitious and had a lot in common. But he was vastly different from Mateo, who had turned into someone she didn't recognize or respect.

She spent the next few weeks trying to convince Jones to let her lead a team back to New York because intel had revealed that operatives were attempting to infiltrate the border. Allegedly, Onyx was the target.

Now that Jones and she were intimate, Onyx believed he wouldn't continue to refuse her request. She was determined to attack first. If they were bold enough to send operatives into Florida, she should return and finish what she started.

Jones was against it and cautioned that this could lead to conflict. Also, now that he and Onyx had gotten entangled, he felt protective, so perhaps her plan had backfired.

However, if they captured operatives illegally entering the border, they could use that to their advantage, "but we cannot make the first move, Onyx," Jones told her while they sat in his kitchen.

Onyx was frustrated. She hated sitting back and waiting for them to attack. "No one knows I work for this government," Onyx said to Jones.

"No," he said, tired of her asking him repeatedly.

"I'm a rogue employee, going back for revenge, which has nothing to do with Florida's government, which is true," Onyx reasoned.

"Onyx, I said no. We are playing chess, not checkers. You can't move on impulse. Wait. Be patient," Jones told her. She sat across from him on the counter, drinking wine.

She rolled her eyes. "Wait, what if they're already here? I could be a sitting duck," she complained.

Onyx had been nagging him for days. "You're not a sitting duck, so don't be dramatic. No one gets across our border undetected. We have the best surveillance technology and hands on deck. So relax," he reassured her.

Onyx wasn't afraid that Kyle sent people over to try to kill her. She only wanted Jones to allow her to go back to kill him.

She poured more wine into her empty glass. "This is ridiculous. We need to be proactive, not reactive. These fucking bastards need to respect us," she instigated.

He laughed. "And they do, but you're being irrational, blinded by your need for revenge," he told her.

He could be correct, but she didn't care. She wanted to go back, and she was going to do so—with or without his support.

He was sitting on a stool drinking wine and smoking a cigar, so she went over and sat atop him, straddled tightly between his body and the counter.

Then as he was exhaling the smoke, she pressed her lips against his and inhaled it, pushing back to exhale the smoke in his face while licking his lips.

"That cigar/wine combination is scrumptious," she said, looking into his eyes.

He put out the cigar and carried her to the bedroom, and she laughed with excitement and eagerness. He quickly threw her on the bed and undressed her. There was nothing about the general she didn't like.

Onyx and Jones spent the following day together. They went shopping and had lunch, and she begged him to take her back to his place. "I want you badly," she said as they ate.

Jones felt alive with Onyx. There was almost nothing he wouldn't do for her. She made him feel like a teenager. Every day with her was an exciting adventure; it had been years since he felt that way.

Losing his wife was tough. They'd been high school sweethearts, and her falling ill was devasting. He would never love another as he did her, but Onyx was undoubtedly a pleasant distraction.

He liked that she wasn't emotional or clingy other than for sex. She did not need to discuss feelings, which was a breath of fresh air. Onyx was what he needed right now.

Onyx was happy too. They understood each other and were compatible, making intimacy much more satisfying and powerful. It was a connection like none she had ever experienced, and she was glad that things turned out the way they did.

The whole purpose of Mateo bringing her here was for her to meet Jones. She felt he was her soul mate. She respected and admired him.

So often, people find themselves in relationships where they do not respect their partner and must force the connection, hoping they can override the fact that they were incompatible. Onyx felt that was the case with Mateo, and she was glad he chose to leave, allowing her to find the perfect mate.

Although only Onyx knew if that was a story, she told it to herself to ease the anger she felt about how Mateo left.

Often, people have a feel-good narrative with which they convince themselves to hide how they truly feel, and usually, trying to persuade others is how they lie to themselves. However, it is only a matter of time before repressed emotions bubble to the surface.

On Monday, Onyx went straight to Ivan's office. She wouldn't take no for an answer, and what Jones didn't know wouldn't hurt him. She preferred to ask for forgiveness than permission.

Since she was a civilian Guard member, she didn't wear a uniform. So this morning, she wore a beige suit with a white tank underneath.

Onyx didn't wear heels because she needed to be comfortable if, as she states, "I need to make a run for it or kick someone's ass."

"Ivan, I want to go on a recon mission to New York. I need a few guys and a passage because if there's a bounty on my head and they can come here to kill me, I should make an unexpected move and strike them at home," she told him confidently, standing by his desk.

Ivan looked at her, uncomfortable. He knew—everyone knew— she was with the general, and thus, she had gained a lot of power and trust in a short period.

There was no reason not to trust Onyx, and Ivan did, but he wasn't sure that a recon mission to New York was something the general meant to do—definitely not one where she was going.

"Onyx, I don't think General Jones wants you to lead a recon mission to New York. He has a lot of people and resources dealing with the threat to your life, and he is taking the matter quite seriously. So please, let us handle it," he said, avoiding eye contact. He didn't like to admit it, but she intimidated him.

Onyx sat, annoyed. "Listen, no one knows their operations or New York as I do, and no one has the training or ability to take on these people like me, so please, don't patronize me. I can handle myself," she told him.

Ivan shook his head. Onyx was challenging to deal with sometimes. She was stubborn and threw a tantrum anytime she didn't get her way.

"Onyx, do what you want. I'll get you some volunteers. But unfortunately, luckily for you, we have many maniacs that would like nothing more than to go on a suicide mission with you," he said, defeated and hoping she would leave him alone.

She's fucking Jones. He won't care, Ivan thought.

She smiled and stood to hug him. "Thank you, thank you, thank you! I won't let you down, I promise. I'll bring you back Kyles's head," she told him excitedly.

Ivan gave Onyx a disgusted look. "Please, leave his head and the rest of his anatomy there," he told her.

She laughed. "Ivan, don't be a little bitch. Grow a pair and get me those volunteers now. I love you. You're the best," she said as she walked out the door.

Onyx had never been this nice to Ivan, but getting what she wanted had perks.

Ivan was glad to see her leave his office; she was like a ticking time bomb. *What the fuck did I do? It will be my head General Jones chops off,* he said to himself, thinking it over.

He couldn't renege on his word, so he quietly began recruiting people to send to New York with Onyx. She would ask him about it daily. "Onyx, I have to set this up with proper planning. I'm working on it," he told her, frustrated a week later.

Onyx knew he was doing this without consulting with Jones, so she tried not to annoy him because if he told Jones about it, the jig was up.

A month later, Onyx asked Jones to move in with her. Ivan was still organizing her trip to New York, and she had mentioned nothing to Jones.

Jones never had children with his deceased wife, and living in that house would probably cause him more pain and prolong the healing process, so he agreed. They didn't hide their relationship at work. Onyx never thought she would be in a relationship like this or live with someone she had fallen hard for. Aside from killing Kyle, there was nothing she wanted more than to be with him.

"I see things are getting serious with you and the general," Ivan said to Onyx one day.

"We are enjoying each other's company," she admitted.

"Well, I heard Sergeant Mercado had a fit when she found out," Ivan said, knowing it would infuriate her.

Onyx shrugged her shoulders, glad Mercado knew that Jones and she were more than a fling.

"Also, she seems happy she will be part of the delegation going to Texas with the general next week," Ivan continued, trying to trigger Onyx.

"Well, I'll be going too," Onyx said stiffly. She was immediately angry. *Why hasn't Jones told me Mercado is going?* she wondered.

"I didn't see your name on the list," Ivan added.

"That's because I'm not going on *official* business," Onyx responded, walking away.

Onyx found herself having fits of jealous rage. Sergeant Mercado was constantly in Jones's office or texting and calling with stupid updates. She was gorgeous and intelligent ... and Onyx hated her.

"That bitch comes to your office way too much. Most of what she has to say can be in an email," Onyx said one day in his office after Mercado left.

She followed Mercado to the door and locked it. Jones laughed. "Are you jealous?" he asked, coming over to where she was standing to hug her.

"I'm not jealous, baby. I'm protective. There's a difference, and she could *never* take my place," she said to him assuredly.

"Call it what you want. It's jealousy," he said to her.

It felt good that she got jealous. Jones enjoyed every time she had a fit because of Mercado. They were very alike, Onyx and Jones.

"Whatever, yes. I'm jealous. Just know I'll cut your dick off," she threatened.

"My love, you're my one and only. So don't be jealous of her or anyone else," Jones told her.

"Oh, and by the way, I'm coming with you on that trip to Texas," she told him.

"Whatever you want, gorgeous," Jones said, caressing her face.

She kissed him and unbuckled his belt. "Onyx, no!" Jones said sternly.

"Oh, baby, please," she pleaded sweetly. "I want you!" She proceeded uncontested.

He liked when she got jealous, but he *loved* how she desired him. It drove him wild, and he probably would go to war for Onyx Pion.

She pulled his pants down to his knees while looking into his eyes. He was as hard as a rock, which excited her. The lust in his eyes made her smile as she took him in.

Then he lifted her onto the desk, and she giggled, eager with anticipation.

Mercado would have Jones over her dead body.

PART TEN

Mateo loved everything about life at Eden. There was something gratifying about rising early and working with a collective to ensure all could eat, have water, and meet their basic needs. He felt invigorated, purposeful, and, most importantly, happy.

Everyone seemed contented and peaceful. There was plenty of time to relax and play, with minimal stress levels and a slow pace. They accomplished everything despite no one being in a rush.

He'd been there almost a year, and he had spent a significant amount of time with Cynthia. They had become very close, in fact.

A few months ago, he expressed his desire to move their relationship to the next level, but Cynthia declined. Instead, she stated that she cared about him deeply. Still, she was not interested in any romantic involvement.

Cynthia's rejection devastated Mateo, but he was glad for her friendship and all she had taught him. She and Nathan were like family, and he was grateful to have them in his life.

Nathan had told him that Karina was interested in getting to know him. She was attractive with a great sense of humor.

Karina taught the younger children and was always kind, so he agreed to get to know her, and to his surprise, he found they had lots in common and got along very well. She was easygoing, and they spent time in nature every day meditating. Cynthia held guided meditations every morning, but sitting in silence was different, and Karina helped him quiet his mind and get better at it.

Mateo was very forthcoming with Karina. He told her he had deep feelings for Cynthia, to which she laughed and stated, "I think we are all in love with Cynthia. I mean, is she even human?"

"She's probably a Pleiadian," Mateo joked, and they laughed.

"Listen, I don't want to get married and have kids. I want to get to know you and have fun. So, what you feel is entirely your business; let's just go with the flow," Karina suggested.

"I like the sound of that," Mateo said.

"Cynthia is too good to be true. People like her only come around once in a lifetime, and if she ever wants to be with you, I'll understand, but life is too short to wait for what may never happen," Karina told him.

Mateo agreed, and they continued laughing. Karina was a breath of fresh air, nonjudgmental, relaxed, and confident. He could tell her anything, and they talked about everything without a problem.

She was nonemotional yet emotionally available. For Mateo, it was just what he needed. She was a massive contrast from Onyx, who, in his opinion, was far too emotional while being emotionally unavailable.

Women are fucking strange, he thought one day as he analyzed it.

Karina took life one day at a time.

Suppose we flow with the current instead of swimming against it? Then life is simple. We choose how we want to feel. But we often stay stuck in our misery because we identify with it, and making a change will alter how we perceive ourselves. Don't take life too seriously. The truth is no one gets out alive. Sometimes, the Universe gives you what you need, not what you want. You only need to be grateful and enjoy life for what it is, making the best of each day. Being alive is a miracle, and you must be thankful for that opportunity.

A few weeks later, Mateo told Carlito he would have a guest in the cabin. "Say no more, brother. I'll get my camping gear, and you can have the cabin to yourselves," he said with a wink and gathered his stuff.

"Thanks," Mateo said, smirking.

He was excited. He pulled out a bottle of wine. They went out into "civilization" weekly for supplies, and he had gotten a few bottles to keep for special occasions. He's been part of the construction and repair team and went for runs with Nathan.

Karina came over. "Oh my, there's wine," she said gleefully.

"I keep a bottle or two for special occasions," he told her.

She smiled. "I'm happy that my visit constitutes a 'special occasion,'" she said, flattered.

He wrapped his arms around her waist. "Yes, it does, beautiful."

It had been a year, and Mateo was in disbelief. *Time flies when you're having fun*, he thought.

"Good morning, sunshine," Karina said to him.

They now shared the cabin. Carlito moved in with his girlfriend, Anna, who was expecting a child.

"Hello, gorgeous," he said, kissing her as she sat beside him on the bed.

"Heading out to teach the future of Eden. Catch you later," she said. Mateo squeezed her thigh as she stood.

"Have a good day, sexy," he said before she shut the door.

He lay back down, feeling grateful. Karina was incredible, and there was no one else he'd rather be with than her.

He dozed off again, suddenly waking to the sound of airboats. "Shit, they're going on a run without me," he exclaimed, jumping out of bed.

He reached the lunch tables and saw Nathan with Cynthia. "Good morning, Hansel and Gretel," Mateo said teasingly.

They laughed at his joke, and Mateo sat to join them.

"Good morning, sleepyhead," Cynthia replied.

As Mateo chatted with Nathan and Cynthia, Carlito came over. "Hey, Mat, Guard soldiers brought a letter for you," he said nervously, and Mateo's stomach sank.

They had no internet, and Cynthia had a cell phone, but the service was poor.

They had permission from the government to settle here, and the Guard had the exact coordinates of their location. They were also required to provide the population growth every six months.

"Thanks, man," Mateo said with a frown.

He was an only child who grew up with a single mother, and she had passed two years before he arrived at Eden. He never met his father, and most of his close friends were there. So, who could be writing him, and about what?

He felt uneasy taking the letter. The envelope had his name written across it. He slowly opened it, trying to guess who could've sent it.

Onyx immediately came to mind.

What now? he thought, finally opening it.

It was from Ivan. Onyx had returned to New York, and he had not heard from her at the scheduled time. He was worried and wanted to know if Mateo could come to assist with locating her. He could be invaluable in her safe return. He also noted that Onyx and the general were an item and that he was willing to go to war to get her back, which could have serious repercussions.

War? Mateo thought.

Of course, that could have a significant impact. If Florida lost, that could affect Eden's way of life. It could mean the return to the union and totalitarianism.

"You have to be fucking kidding me," he said when he had finished reading it.

"What's the matter?" Cynthia asked, concerned.

Mateo rested his head in his hands and massaged his temples. He could not allow Onyx to destroy what he had here. He couldn't let her mess up things more than they already were.

"Something has come up. I have to go back into civilization for a few days, possibly back to New York," Mateo said, anguished.

Nathan looked alarmed. "What? Bro, weren't they like looking to kill you because of that girl? So why would you go back there?" he asked.

Mateo sighed. "Because that same girl has gone back and could cause a war," he said.

Cynthia took his hand. "Mateo, you don't owe anyone anything. Your duty is to yourself. Everything else will work itself out. People are free to choose but never free from the consequences of their choices. Your friend made a choice. You rescued her once before at a great cost. You have something good here; don't jeopardize your life and well-being for people who care only for themselves," she said, reasoning with him.

He squeezed her hand. "The truth is, I don't think this is a request. I fear I have 'been summoned,' and I'm not doing this for her. I am doing it for you, Nathan, Carlito, Karina, and everyone who lives here in peace," he told her.

Mateo returned to his cabin to pack a bag, having made up his mind. He anxiously waited for Karina, and when she got home, he showed her the letter. As she read it, he explained that he had to see Ivan to help him bring Onyx back and prevent an all-out war that could threaten their way of life.

She was reticent, and Mateo didn't know what else to say, so he opened the bag he had packed to ensure he didn't forget anything.

"I support whatever you feel you need to do, but please don't say you're doing this for us or for peace. Please don't insult my intelligence. You're doing this for her, for Onyx. She has a hold on you, and you can run to the ends of the earth, but if she calls, you go running back," she said after a long while.

Mateo didn't answer. Onyx was his responsibility. He brought her here. He left her to join the Guard, seduce the powerful, and cause havoc.

He wished he had refused to help her and come here, leaving her to her fate. But he was sure she would've managed fine without him, and he realized she had used him.

Onyx didn't give a shit about him. She just wanted him to help her get out of the mess she was in, the same way she was using the Guard and General Jones to accomplish her goals … a means to an end, with no regard for anything but herself and her needs.

She was the personification of selfishness, and Mateo finally wished to have her out of his life. She epitomized everything he hated about people, and he loathed that she had manipulated him into this shit, but how do you explain that to someone?

There was no way Karina would understand. Despite her easygoing personality, this was beyond what she could comprehend. He held her tightly and said, "Thank you for your unconditional love and support. I love you," he told her.

Love is a narrow concept, the way it is defined. People believe it is an unconscious impulse when it is a choice. You have yet to understand that you must love what is good for you and who is best for you. How much heartache it would save …

I loved Onyx but understood she was not good for me, so I decided to walk away. Now, I feel like a black hole is pulling me back to her. It's like a curse, Mateo thought, aggravated.

How often do people in the same situation hold on in the name of love … loving another to the extent that they stop loving themselves? That is not love. That is capriciousness. It is everything, ultimately about choice, down to the last detail. You are, indeed, free to choose but never free from the consequences of your choices.

I love Cynthia, but that love is unrequited, so I made a different choice. Karina. She is the right choice. She is good to me and good for me. She brings me peace, happiness, and love. The choice is always mine. I either choose to be miserable or find the people and things that complement my happiness because looking for happiness outside myself is pointless. I can only share my joy. How could I ever surrender the power of my happiness to another? Most people can't even be happy within themselves, yet we expect them to make us happy. What a tragedy, Mateo thought, unable to sleep.

Tomorrow, someone would pick him up to meet Ivan. Mateo's head was spinning, and he didn't want to leave. He wanted to stay here with Karina. He was happy, and he felt hatred for the first time.

I hate you, Onyx Pion, he thought.

He was off early. "I'll be back before you know it," he said, kissing Karina.

"Please, be careful," she said worriedly, hugging him tightly.

The whole ride, Mateo felt nauseated. Eden was his home. He didn't want to leave the people he loved, those who cared about him, because of Onyx.

One thing Mateo was sure of; he would die to ensure that no harm ever came to Eden.

Guardsmen escorted Mateo to Ivan's office as soon as he arrived. "Man, am I glad to see you," Ivan said, patting Mateo's back. "How are you?" he asked Mateo, motioning him to sit.

"I was doing remarkably well until I received your letter," Mateo said as he sat.

Ivan sat with a look of anguish on his face. "I messed up, Mat, but she is relentless and annoying. She got me to get some guys to go with her to New York. She claimed it was for recognizance, but I know it is all for her to get revenge. The worst part is the general told her no. I knew he didn't want her to go, but I wasn't sure he had said no. Onyx has him wrapped around her finger, so I thought it was no big deal. After all, Onyx gets what she wants."

Ivan continued rambling on about Onyx, her tantrums, and the general being infuriated with him for assisting her with this mission. Not once did he mention that he was upset with her. So obviously, the general was blaming Ivan for her decision to go … classic Onyx manipulation.

"Why am I here, Ivan? What do you want from me? I have a life, and I'd like to return to it. I'm sick and tired of Onyx and her bullshit, and honestly, if I never see her again, I'm cool with that, so please, tell me what you need from me," Mateo asked, annoyed. He felt anger rising. So much for meditation, oneness, and good stuff. Yet, he was in the real world, furious for the first time in a year.

He had not been angry in three hundred and sixty-five days, give or take a few, yet Onyx marched back into his life, causing a relapse of anger and frustration.

"Truthfully, when you wrote and said you would come, I was elated, but I had already heard from her," Ivan admitted.

Mateo interrupted. "So, you mean to tell me I came for no reason? You wrote back with all the arrangements; you could've told me to disregard," Mateo said, visibly irritated.

Ivan shook his head before the words left his mouth. "No, we still wanted you to be here, just in case. I know you can provide us with information if we need to send an extraction team for them," Ivan told him.

Now the anger turned into rage. "You're telling me that Onyx is OK somewhere in New York, playing vigilante, but you *still* called me here, *just in case*? Did I get that right?" Mateo asked.

Ivan nodded remorsefully. In his defense, this was the general's idea. However, Ivan didn't think that Mateo would be this upset.

Mateo stood up and began to pace back and forth. "You people think I'm at your beck and call? I have a life, Ivan!" he yelled. "I can't believe you brought me back here because Onyx is a spoiled fucking brat, and daddy is letting her get away with literal murder!" he shouted.

Ivan was stunned, but there was nothing he could say. He was nervous. He had already fucked up with Onyx. The general would not tolerate it if Mateo left. The general had explicitly stated that he wanted Mateo to assist with her safe return, and if he stormed out, Ivan knew there was no getting him back. He could not allow Mateo to leave, but keeping him against his will was not exactly an option. Well, desperate times call for desperate measures. Nevertheless, he was sure Mateo would forgive him if it came down to it.

Ivan had to look out for himself. But of course, it was Mateo's fault. After all, *he* brought the femme fatale here, and whether he wanted to or not, Ivan would make him clean up her mess.

PART ELEVEN

General Jones was expecting Ivan. He had scheduled a meeting for nine that morning, but Ivan had rescheduled for the afternoon. He was furious but agreed. Ivan alleged that he was sorting out intel from New York so that he could give him the most accurate, up-to-date information.

Sergeant Mercado knocked and entered before Jones could beckon her in.

"Sir, we have some important updates from the border," she said, walking over to his desk and coming around to where he was seated to show him images on a tablet.

Jones took the tablet from her, and she leaned in closer. He could smell she was wearing a pleasant floral perfume.

"We're not sure who they are, but they crossed over at approximately 0200 hours. We have a team in pursuit, attempting to gather intelligence. I decided it was best to follow than apprehend. That way, they can lead us to their contacts on our side. We are tracking their every movement. I want to know what their plan is," she told him.

"Excellent work, Sergeant. That was a great call."

He was preoccupied with the Onyx situation but was glad he had competent and reliable people like Mercado handling other vital issues.

Sergeant Mercado placed a hand on General Jones's shoulder. "Is there anything else I can assist with? I know a classified mission is taking place, but if there is anything I can do, please let me know," she said, and he looked up at her, placing his hand over hers.

"No, thank you, Esperanza. You are one of my best, and precisely what you are doing is what I need you to do—nothing else. Now, if there's nothing else, I have an urgent matter to see to," he told her dismissively.

She removed her hand from his shoulder and headed for the door. She hesitated before leaving, looked back, and said: "Sir!"

He looked up and saw her halfway out the door. "Yes?" he asked.

She pressed her lips, pondering what she was going to say. "I just hope you know what you are doing," she said with concern.

"I have everything under control, Mercado," he said confidently.

"Good," she said, quietly shutting the door.

That cunt has him blinded, doing reckless shit and wasting valuable resources while we have serious problems here, Mercado thought angrily, walking to her office.

Onyx was wearing a hooded sweatshirt and cargo pants. They had been following Steve for a few days now. She had a source that gave her his information. So she followed him and kept a chronological log of his daily routine.

She had seen Kyle on more than one occasion, and although she wanted to shoot him in the head where he stood each time, she managed to subdue the urge.

Kyle had extensive security detail, and his variable schedule made his moves hard to predict, which is why Onyx focused on Steve.

Now that she was here, Onyx was more ambitious with her plan. She wanted the big fish, Simon, and Steve was the key to getting to him.

"How much longer are we going to be here?" Pinky asked.

Onyx rolled her eyes. Ivan only allowed her to bring five volunteers, three of whom were tailing people on her orders, and she was stuck with two morons she nicknamed Pinky and the Brain.

"Listen, Pinky, you wanted to be here. So, why aren't you having fun?" she asked, sticking her tongue out at him.

"You said we were going to get some action, and all we've been doing is following this fucktard around," he complained.

She smiled at him. "What kind of action do you have in mind, Pinky?" she asked flirtatiously.

He blushed. "The kind I can use my gun on, babe," he said to her, grabbing the gun holstered on his belt.

"I promise you'll use that gun; just be patient," she assured him.

I can't believe he stuck me with these two idiots, Onyx thought, now, sure that Ivan deliberately gave her the bottom of the barrel.

She turned around to face the backseat. "You good, Brain? You're always so serious," she said to the brain sitting in the back.

"I'm good, just hungry," he whined.

I'm with two fucking infants, she thought and laughed.

"When are you *not* hungry? You'd eat a horse if you could. Remind me never to have kids," she said.

They both shrugged their shoulders like disgruntled teenagers.

"We're almost done. What do you say we go to the strip club after this?" she asked, hoping to cheer them up.

They both nodded. She had promised a wild adventure, and so far, they had spent their days in absolute boredom, and Ivan kept pressuring her to wrap it up and get back, but she was here. Although she was happy with the Guard, she often felt bored. Being here was exhilarating, and thinking of the look on Kyle's face when she finally faced him was what kept her going.

Jones was livid, and she was doing her best to stay in his good graces. Onyx found that face-watching naked helped, but she wasn't sure that would last.

There was only so much phone sex they could have. Onyx was beginning to worry she was running out of time. Even the other team members seemed to want to go back to Florida. So she had to think of something fast.

She had instructed the three following Kyle's low-level operatives to terminate the targets once they had the information she wanted to keep them motivated. To her surprise, she found hesitation. "Get it done," she said coldly. "*That's* why we're here," she insisted.

Did they think the action was coming via virtual reality? Unfortunately, people are so used to the virtual world that they can't function in real life.

Pinky shifted in his seat to face her. "How come they get all the action?" he asked, aggravated.

She placed her hand on his upper thigh. "Baby, I promise we will have the *best* action," she said, winking, and he moved her hand further up.

"Don't tease me with a good time," Pinky joked.

Onyx squeezed. "I *never* tease!" Then she pulled her hand back and laughed.

Soon after, they saw Steve exit the building they were watching.

"Steve is on the move. Let's go. If Kyle is meeting him, we'll take them both out. *That* will send Simon a message," Onyx instructed.

They followed Steve, but it did not appear he was meeting with anyone from Orion. He had left the city and crossed into Westchester County. They had kept a close eye on him, but he had never left the town before. He had an apartment in Lower Manhattan, and as far as they knew, he lived alone. Then Steve took a new route, a break in his routine, so she asked Pinky to follow.

"It's Friday. Maybe he has a wife and kids in the suburbs, and the sidepiece probably lives downtown. So he leaves in the evenings, and we haven't seen him," the brain said.

"That's why you're the brains of this operation," Onyx said, looking back at him. "That's how you do it?" she asked, still watching him.

"Do what?" Pinky asked, confused.

"And that's why you're a moron if that's how *you* cheat on *your* wife, genius. By setting up the side chick in an apartment? You men are pieces of shit and can never be trusted." She continued without awaiting his response.

Meanwhile, Ivan was tapping his leg and biting his nails. He was a nervous wreck. Mateo had stormed out of his office exactly as he feared the day before, and Ivan had been calling his hotel room but had not been able to speak with him.

This is bad, really bad. Ivan had managed to postpone the morning meeting, but he needed to confirm that Mateo was here and ready to assist them with finding Onyx.

Ivan called the hotel front desk a third time, and the receptionist assured him Mateo had not checked out but was not in his room and that she would give him the message as soon as he returned.

Once he had ended the call, he took a deep breath. Ivan felt as though a hand had been squeezing his neck, restricting the airflow, and he could finally breathe ... a little. The anxiety was killing him.

After his run, Mateo went back to the hotel to shower.

"Excuse me, Mr. Martinez." Mateo turned to see the receptionist holding a piece of paper. "I have a message for you," she told him.

He doubled back to the front desk, having already walked by it. "Thank you," he said politely.

He read the note. "*Call Ivan immediately,*" it read. He crumbled the piece of paper and put it in his pocket. *The nerve of these fucking people. They expect me to sit around this hotel for God knows how long, waiting to see if the she-devil returns in one piece*, Mateo thought, aggravated.

Ivan said he should stick around. Mateo had left his office without an answer. He knew Ivan must be pissing in his pants. *Good for him. Let him explain it to the general*, he thought, amused.

He took a shower and immediately thought of Onyx. The last time he was in this hotel, they had taken an exhilarating shower together. It felt like a lifetime ago. We can be intricately close to people one day and become strangers the next, dancing between contempt and yearning.

Karina would not be happy when he told her he would be here until further notice, and Cynthia would be disappointed.

When he got out of the shower, he called Ivan. "What's the emergency?" he asked, irritated. "You keep calling as if my mother died," he said reproachfully.

"Are you still here?" Ivan asked in a whimper.

"Yes, I am. So, what do you want?" Mateo asked angrily.

Ivan began to stutter. "I-I just-um, like, are you, I-I mean, you-you sticking around?" he managed to ask.

Mateo took a deep breath. "Yes, bro, I am. Do I have to be in that building too?" he asked, exasperated.

There was a long pause, "If you don't mind," Ivan finally said. "General Jones would like to see you," he confessed.

Mateo was silent. *He wants to see me? Really? What is there to say? His psycho girlfriend is up in New York, saving the day. What the hell does that have to do with me?* he thought.

"When?" Mateo asked.

"Two this afternoon," Ivan said, shaking.

"I'll be there," Mateo said, hanging up.

Ivan was outside the building when Mateo arrived, and Mateo felt guilty. Ivan looked stressed and worried.

Not too long ago, Mateo was in his shoes, crippled by anxiety, sinking into a hole dug out by Onyx.

"Hey, man," said Ivan, nodding.

Mateo stood in front of him and placed a hand on his shoulder. "Listen, I'm sorry. I've been acting like a jerk," Mateo told him apologetically.

Ivan relaxed a little. Having Mateo angry with him and everything else gave him an ulcer.

"I know you're under a lot of pressure, and I know that dealing with this Onyx situation is more than you can handle. I accept it is my fault for bringing her here. You stuck your neck out for me, and since arriving, she's been nothing but trouble. I'll do whatever you need me to do to make it right," he assured Ivan.

Ivan smiled with relief. "No, she has done more good than harm. She *is* an asset, but her need for revenge and inability to follow orders or take constructive criticism is the problem. However, we feel once she can overcome those things, all will be fine," Ivan told him.

It seems Ivan too was under the Onyx spell.

Mateo laughed. "The only way she will overcome that is by killing Kyle and saving the world after that. There will *always* be something she will want to do and someone to defy," Mateo warned him.

They walked into the building, signed in, and went straight to the general's office.

"You sitting in?" Mateo asked Ivan.

"Should I?" Ivan asked, concerned, "I can only deal with one lunatic at a time, not two," he said, opening the door to General Jones's office.

"Sir, Mateo is here," Ivan announced.

Mateo walked into the office as Ivan held open the door, and once he had stepped in, Ivan left.

Ivan was sure that Jones wanted him there, but Mateo didn't know that, and Ivan doubted he would call him back.

"Sir," Mateo said, shaking his hand.

"Sit," Jones said, taking his seat.

Mateo sat.

"Would you like a cigar?" he asked Mateo, lighting one up.

"No," Mateo said, looking up at the fire alarm.

"It's disabled," Jones replied, following his gaze.

Mateo nodded.

"Some things are inevitable. I'll either burn here or burn in hell. Either way, I'm going to burn," Jones said. He blew out the smoke and asked Mateo if he wanted a drink, but Mateo refused.

"A man with no vice is a powerful man. Self-control requires more willpower than controlling others," he said, studying Mateo.

"I agree, but we all have our weaknesses," Mateo admitted.

Jones smiled and replied, "Yes, some more than others."

"Indeed," Mateo agreed, thinking, *Some vices can get you killed.*

"What are the odds that Onyx comes back alive?" he asked immediately. Mateo was relieved because he hated small talk. He already wanted this meeting to be over.

"Forty percent, and I only say that because she has the element of surprise. She is way over her head," Mateo said frankly.

Jones took another pull from the cigar. "I see," he said, exhaling smoke.

Mateo watched him take another pull from the cigar and followed it with a shot of whisky.

"I figured that much. I warned Onyx not to go, but she is an obstinate woman. She is too young to understand that some things require fineness, that a chess game can take many years *and* great loss before the checkmate," Jones said to Mateo.

Mateo sat quietly; he was unsure where he was going with this.

"We often must make huge sacrifices for the greater good. The simplest solution for this problem would be to let the events play out without interference, whatever the cost, wouldn't you agree?" he asked Mateo.

Does he mean to leave her to her fate?

"I'm not sure I understand what you mean," Mateo responded.

"Oh, but you do. So let me ask you, would you be willing to risk your life and lead an extraction team to find Onyx?" he asked.

I get it, Mateo thought. *We are all pieces on a chessboard, some valuable and others expendable.*

"He isn't interested in causing conflict to get her back. She can die in New York for all he cares; the trash takes out itself, but he enjoys his toy. I don't blame him," Mateo said to himself.

That's the thing with vices. They control you.
"I would," Mateo said, aware that he was the expendable piece.

PART TWELVE

Onyx woke up hungover the following day. The stint at the strip club went on longer than she expected, but it was fun. She did not remember having this much fun in a long time—if ever. Her fun memories were all with Mateo, and they were not as exciting.

She realized a lot she had not experienced and felt sad for all she had missed out on, like prom, school trips, a best friend, a high school sweetheart, underage drinking, sleepovers, and everyday life for many.

"Shit, it's late!" she yelled from the couch where she was sleeping. Pinky and the brain were on separate twin-sized beds in the same hotel room.

"Get up, you fucking degenerates. We have shit to do," Onyx shouted, going over and shaking them.

"What time is it?" asked Pinky, eyes still shut.

"Time to get the fuck up," Onyx replied and went into the bathroom to shower.

She had decided she was going to take out Kyle and Steve. But Simon was no easy target; in retrospect, she had already missed out on many things. She wanted to return to Jones and enjoy her new life with him, do more exciting things, and focus less on work.

"I'm hungry," the brain said. The brain was driving today because Pinky was complaining of a headache. Pinky always complained about something.

"We need to eat if we're going on a … well, you know," he said, and Pinky and Onyx laughed.

"Can't do anything on an empty stomach," said Pinky from the passenger seat.

Onyx was riding in the backseat, thinking about everything she wanted to do when she returned to Florida. Like dancing. She thought, *I want to go dancing, but do I even know how to dance?*

"Onyx!" Pinky shouted, turning around, bringing her out of contemplation.

"What?" she asked, annoyed.

"What's for breakfast?" he asked. "New York is your turf."

She looked out the car window to see where they were. "There's a diner on the next block. Stop there," she suggested.

They sat at a booth and ordered. The brain asked Onyx what the plan was, discussing it as they ate.

"You two understand?" she asked after explaining the plan a second time.

"Yeah, we got it," Brain said, eating a piece of bacon and gulping down some coffee.

"Good, because we only get one shot at this. If we fuck this up, we're dead," Onyx reminded them.

They nodded in agreement with mouths full, and Onyx took a bite from the last piece of banana walnut pancake on her plate and washed it down with black coffee. Her face would be the last thing Kyle saw, and if she had it her way, she would make him take her to Simon to finish the job.

Word on the street was that Kyle was only still breathing because Simon was hopeful that he would find and kill Onyx. What satisfaction it would give her to take out both of them.

She just hoped Dumb and Dumber didn't mess things up. Finally, they left the diner. Steve was the first target. They had sufficient information on him, and deducing exactly where to find him at this time would be easy.

Steve was a creature of habit. His daily routine made his days virtually identical. Kyle was more erratic. He seemed to operate more on impulse than on preparation. Kyle didn't plan out his days, so she would use Steve to get more information; Kyle's little pet must know where he lived.

Orion hierarchy was very secretive, and personnel assignment was confidential information, but they knew more of each other at the top.

Steve didn't have a significant security detail. *Getting to him will be easy*, she thought. Now, she felt a sense of urgency. All she could think of was getting back to Jones. Ironic how a change in perspective can instantaneously shift importance in our lives.

"Stop here," Onyx instructed the brain.

They were a few streets away from Steve's Westchester County house, outside the city, a rather impressive piece of property in Scarsdale.

He arrived late at night, and they only recently discovered it because he had come before his usual time. It was Saturday, and he had come up early. Onyx did not want to stop in front. It would raise suspicion.

The city is different. People go about their business, not paying attention or caring about what is happening. But here, they would stand out. Everyone is aware of one another. A strange car was going to raise some brows, so they should not stand there long.

They were tailing Steve, and he had stopped at a liquor store. Onyx thought they should keep going. He had to pass this street to get home.

She was uncertain what type of security system he had, so breaking in and risking getting caught or captured on a live feed would hurt her plan. She opted to wait. She was going to ambush him as he went into the house.

She told Pinky and Brain to wait outside. She could handle this on her own. She only needed the lookout and getaway.

Steve's phone rang before he reached his car. It was Kyle. "Hey, what's up?" he asked.

"There has been a development. Can you come to see me?" Kyle asked.

Steve shook his head. "Man, I'm a few minutes away from home. Can this wait?" he complained.

Kyle grunted. "You've been compromised, so I wouldn't go home if I were you," Kyle warned him.

"What the hell you talking about?" Steve asked, looking around and suddenly running to his car and locking the door.

"I've had techs running face rec software around the clock since that bitch got out, and she has unexpectedly resurfaced. We've seen her in your vicinity on multiple occasions. I believe you have a tail," Kyle warned him.

Steve turned his head to look behind him. He was nervous. "How long have you known, and why me? Shouldn't she be after you?" Steve asked.

Kyle laughed. "Because you're stupid, and I'm not, that's why. Onyx thinks if she goes after you, then she'll get to me," Kyle said.

"Right," Steve said, wounded. He was sure that Kyle's arrogance would one day get the best of him. He felt like going home and striking a deal with Onyx. Steve would gladly give him up, but he did not know if she would be interested, so he decided against it.

"So, what's the plan?" Steve asked Kyle dully.

"Come see me. I've already dispatched a team to your place," Kyle informed him. He promised they would bring Onyx to Orion if she's there, where he'll end this.

Fuck! Simon should've killed Kyle when she got away, and she would have never returned. Now, she's back, and there's no telling what kind of shitstorm she has planned, Steve thought bitterly.

"Be there soon. Oh, please tell your imbeciles not to destroy my place," Steve said to Kyle.

"Can't make promises I can't keep, Steve," Kyle said, ending the call.

Onyx was getting anxious. *He should've arrived by now. Where the fuck is he?* she thought.

"Shouldn't he have been here by now?" said Pinky, infuriating Onyx.

She wasn't one to get angry, but this was absurd. "Thanks for stating the obvious, Sherlock," she said coolly.

He knows. Kyle knows I'm here, Onyx thought.

Orion has too much tech and surveillance, and she has wasted too much time. *He must've warned Steve. Fuck, I should've made my move sooner*, she thought.

Onyx had a subpar piece of tracking tech on Steve's car, but she didn't need it. The problem wasn't finding Kyle now. The issue was getting into Orion headquarters ... alive.

Steve arrived at Orion headquarters in downtown Manhattan sweating, although it was chilly outside. He was nervous and continued to look over his shoulder even after passing through security.

"This is fucking ridiculous, Kyle. I don't understand why that bitch is after me. She could've killed me," Steve told him, scared.

Kyle roared with laughter. He found pleasure in Steve's weakness. If Simon only knew. *Is this the little bitch he's willing to replace me with?* he thought.

Kyle was aware of Simon's plan. He had a lot of loyal friends within the organization and was preparing for a quiet takeover. He had a powerful ally in one of their biggest clients, Mosk, the owner of Space Linkage Conglomerate. Space Linkage colonized Mars, and Mosk planned to leave for Mars himself, but first, he wanted Kyle to be the head of Orion, a company Mosk founded but then sold.

When Mateo said Onyx was in over her head, he didn't realize it was a prophetic statement. Kyle had allied himself with absolute power and will sit on the throne, and once that happens, Onyx will not stand a chance.

"Relax, my friend; sit. Let me get you a drink," Kyle said to Steve, shoving him into a chair.

Steve was no longer nervous. Now, he was afraid. "You know Simon expects a phone call from me within the hour," he told Kyle.

Kyle handed Steve a drink. "Cheers," Kyle said, raising his glass and drinking its content in one gulp.

With trembling hands, Steve took the glass from Kyle and downed it as well. However, his vision blurred within seconds, and his tongue went numb. He tried to speak but couldn't. Finally, attempting to stand, he fell off the chair, and immediately, his bowels and bladder loosened, and a soupy brown mixture puddled under him and quickly spread out.

"That, my friend," said Kyle crouching over him, "is a synthetic platypus-cone snail venom. The scientists at Pharma Corp have been developing amazing things. First, it paralyzes, and then you'll experience a slow, agonizing death," Kyle told a slobbering Steve and spat at him before standing again.

"You and Simon thought you could outsmart me, but his mistake was not killing me when he had the chance. Your mistake was thinking you would live to see my demise," Kyle said with sinister laughter.

Steve had terrible spasms as he lay on the floor, praying for a quick death. Kyle looked down at him, disgusted, and leaned forward. "I haven't even told you the *best* part yet," he said excitedly.

Steve's face contorted with excruciating pain, but he could not make a sound.

"Your fearless leader is headed to a summit at the UN. Mosk will name those he will leave in charge when he goes off-planet, but unfortunately, Simon's Tespa electric car will explode before he can get there," Kyle said with a menacing laugh.

"What that piece of shit Simon doesn't know is that this plan is already in motion, and there's a fail-safe. If something happens to Simon, *I* will be in command," Kyle confessed to Steve with mirth.

Steve's eyes widened, and Kyle kicked him.

"*I* will be the king, you little piece of shit, and rule with an iron fist. I have absolute power, and I *will* find Onyx Pion and gut her like a pig!" Kyle exclaimed triumphantly.

The office phone rang, and Kyle rushed to answer it. "Sir, there has been a terrible accident. You must present yourself at the United Nations," the woman said to Kyle.

"What sort of accident?" he asked, hiding his excitement.

"Sir, you will be briefed when you arrive, but you must arrive forthwith," she insisted.

Kyle smiled. He was already wearing his best suit and had a fresh haircut and a facial.

"I'll be right there," he told the woman.

He walked over to Steve as he buttoned his jacket. Steve was convulsing on the floor.

"I didn't cut you up and feed you to the pigs because I didn't want to get my suit dirty. So, you should be grateful," Kyle said, leaving Steve a horrific and slow death.

PART THIRTEEN

Mateo sat in Ivan's office. They didn't say much to each other, and Mateo was praying for this to end soon. He missed Eden. He missed nature, his friends, and Karina. He missed working with his hands and, most of all, the simplicity of life there.

Here, everything is so complex. No one is who they appear to be, and everyone has a self-serving agenda motivated by their ego. Mateo shifted in his chair, lost in his thoughts.

At Eden, we all work together for the benefit of all, and collective well-being is paramount. The contrast is evident. Jones talks about a greater good, but who benefits from this greater good? Is it not a select few and not "the whole"? Mateo asked himself, taking apart a pen. *If it were the whole, there wouldn't be so much chaos, or maybe we aren't meant to live like this, so many of us condensed in one place. Perhaps, we should be living in small settlements like Eden. But instead, they lie, they tell us the world is overpopulated, but that is not true,* he told himself, throwing the now-broken pen in the trash.

There is just too many people in a select number of cities worldwide. The rest of the planet is empty. They make it uncomfortable and impossible for people to survive and thrive outside the script. Had they developed Nikola Tesla's technologies, we would be using free, clean energy globally. Mateo was lost in thought as he now stood and looked out the window.

They'll tell us that it is not possible, all while claiming they want our best, the alleged greater good—lies upon lies. They want people mentally and physically ill, consuming and working for their benefit, not the greater good, he thought, getting upset.

Now he sounded like Onyx. When under pressure, people either break down or free themselves. As with all things, it is a matter of choice.

113

He was at a crossroads, uncertain if what he was doing was the right choice. Couldn't he leave and return to Eden, or would they track him down and bring him back against his will?

Mateo wasn't sure what to think anymore. He was sure he couldn't trust the general. *And what's the holdup anyway?* he thought anxiously.

"Any word today?" Mateo asked Ivan while folding his arms and biting his lower lip.

Ivan typed something on his computer. "Actually, yes. Onyx wrote an encrypted message. She said they are a go for today," he said, still typing.

Mateo paced from the window to the door, thinking. *What does that mean exactly? What is her plan, and can she pull it off without getting killed? What is the purpose of an extraction team? Shouldn't we already be there?*

He wasn't eager to return to New York, but in the case of an extraction, there must be some sense of urgency, so unless they were going in to extract corpses, they should have already been on their way—shouldn't they?

The anticipation was killing him, and just as he was about to sit down, Jones walked in. "Oh good, you're both here," he said and shut the door.

Mateo stood straight and expectantly waited for the general to say what he had come to say.

"The mission is a go. We've activated the extraction team. You leave now," he said, looking at Mateo.

Careful what you wish for, Mateo thought, and his stomach started to cramp. The nervousness was paralyzing, and he stood frozen.

Ivan jumped out of his seat. "Sir, do you have all the particulars so I can assemble a team?" Ivan asked. He was shocked. He assumed his task would have been the team selection, and he would've had a little more time.

"No need, Ivan. I have handpicked this team myself. I have all the particulars in this folder," Jones said and handed Ivan the folder he held.

"You will be leading a team of five, including Mateo here. The others are ready and awaiting your instructions," Jones told Ivan and opened the door to leave.

Ivan's jaw hit the floor. He was in utter disbelief and overcome with fear.

"Ivan," Jones said before departing, "that file is classified. It was prepared by me, for your eyes only," Jones warned him.

Ivan nodded with understanding. "Yes, sir," he mumbled, trying to regain his composure.

"Good luck; bring her back," Jones said, shutting the door behind him.

"I guess I'm not the only disposable piece after all," Mateo said cynically, and Ivan turned to look at him, bewildered.

"Oh, you thought you would be sitting here comfortably hiding behind your computer while I led a team to New York to fetch the general's plaything?" Mateo asked Ivan, laughing.

"My place is where the general needs me. I'm the only one he trusts," Ivan said softly.

"Yeah, he trusts you more than me, but if you were such a valuable right hand, he wouldn't send you off, and certainly not as a surprise, but what the fuck do I know?" Mateo said.

"Let's go. Let's get this shit over with," Ivan snapped.

They found the rest of the crew and jumped into a van that transported them to the airport. Everything was happening so fast that Mateo could barely process it.

They arrived in New York on a small, chartered plane. Although the relationship between the now-separate countries was superficially friendly, every attempt at coup d'état had been made, with the US alleging that rogue Union advocates were to blame.

Never in the past year had Mateo imagined himself being back here. But Cynthia always said, "We attract what we fear," which was true because the thought of returning to New York was dreadful—and now, here he was.

Mateo took his bag from the crew member outside the aircraft. He wondered what the status was with Onyx and her team. Hopefully, they could link up and fly back to Florida together because a confrontation with Orion, the top security contractor in the world, was not something he wanted to happen.

Not my fight, he thought, but a voice in his head said, *Yes, it is. The moment you involved yourself, it became your fight, or did you forget* you *shot Kyle?* Mateo shook it off and followed Ivan and the rest of the team.

Ivan was still stunned he was leading this team. Mateo felt he was more of an administrative type than hands-on, so he was trying to understand why the general handpicked him for this task.

Was it because he was the only person he trusted? Or because he was a loose end? And why is the file for his eyes only? Ivan had already discussed most of its contents with the team. The file contained the pedigree of all members assigned to the extraction team, contact points, vehicle information, flight itineraries, hotel arrangements, and so on.

Or was there something else that Ivan was withholding and pretending to share all the contents to give them a false sense of security?

Mateo's head was spinning. He noticed Ivan was jittery, possibly because of his nerves. Of course, he was no field agent.

Regardless, Mateo was uneasy. He knew Ivan and considered him a friend, but as the general once said, all is fair in love and war, and you never truly know people.

The others were quiet and serious. No one had said much, only asked questions pertinent to the mission. They were focused and appeared calm, which was comforting because Ivan was nervous, and Mateo was apprehensive because he knew what they were against with Orion and Kyle.

Onyx was unaware of their arrival, and she didn't even know Mateo was collaborating with the Guard to bring her back.

"Did you reach out to Onyx to see if there is anything she needs us to do?" Mateo asked Ivan.

"Only the general has contact with her, and he did not inform her of the plan because he feared she might interpret it as something else. He didn't want her to think she could openly engage Orion," Ivan admitted.

Orion may be a private organization, but they had deep ties with the government through all their black ops contracts involving the military, and the general did not want that kind of conflict.

"So, how will we know how to find them, or if they need our help?" Mateo asked Ivan, confused.

"We get our orders directly from General Jones. He is tracking Onyx, and they maintain contact, so if she needs anything, she will contact him, and he will relay that to us," Ivan informed him.

Mateo shook his head with frustration. "That is a complete waste of time. By the time we get the message, they could all be dead," he said, annoyed.

Ivan turned to face Mateo and said, "If you ask me, that sounds like a problem solved!"

They stared at each other for a while without saying a word. Mateo wasn't sure how he felt about Ivan's comment, and before he could decipher his thoughts, the woman who was part of the team interrupted them. "You two going to kiss, or can we get moving?" she asked condescendingly.

As Onyx suspected, Steve was at Orion headquarters in the city, complicating things. There was no way she was getting in there now that they knew she was in the vicinity. The whole plan had gone to shit, and she thought, *I should just take the loss and go back to Florida before they track us down.*

"They're on to us. Steve is at Orion. We need to return this car and get another one. They probably have the plate number," she advised the other two.

The brain turned the car around. "Let's return it here in Westchester," Pinky suggested.

"Good idea, Pinky. Let me send a message so that another is set aside for us. You can go in and retrieve the keys," Onyx told him.

Onyx found the nearest car rental and directed Brain there. Then finally, she got a response from Jones. He instructed her to acquire the new vehicle and get out.

There was a chartered plane waiting for them. Jones sent the location, and she considered it. She had lost this fight. She could always come back. Now, she knew Jones would not leave her here, that he would help her get out, so she could fight another day ... Only she could not. She had to do something. Kyle would not expect her to come a hundred feet from headquarters.

They were getting a new vehicle. Onyx and the morons would wait outside for Steve and make a move then. Onyx was not going to leave empty-handed.

They got the new ride. "What now?" asked Brain.

"We go to Orion and wait for Steve to leave unless he is too scared and plans to sleep there. Then maybe we'll get lucky and catch Kyle instead," she said, smiling and rubbing her hands together.

"Why don't we just go to his apartment, break in, and wait for him inside?" Pinky asked.

Onyx rested her head on the car seat. "Because it's probably under constant surveillance and full of tech. He probably has motion sensors all over that place. If Brain's theory is true, he probably has cameras in every room, including the bathroom, because he can't have the sidepiece bringing in men while he's gone like he does with women," she answered.

Onyx closed her eyes. *Why am I doing this?* she asked herself.

Mateo was right. It doesn't matter what I do. Nothing will change. I take Kyle out, and someone else takes his place. I bring down Orion and Pharma Corp, and the competitors move to the top. Who am I kidding? No one will appreciate it. Hell, they will probably villainize me as a traitor, terrorist, or enemy of the state! The sheep don't want to be enlightened. They want to "be woke." Who am I to change that which they love? They deserve this wretched world they created. I am risking my life for what? I won't even be a martyr. I'll be another dead conspiracy theorist, and no one will miss me—not Mateo, not Jones, certainly not Ivan, and not these two morons—no one, she told herself.

"We're here, sunshine. Wakey, wakey," said Pinky, parking across the street from Orion headquarters.

They waited for hours. Steve, it seemed, was too afraid to leave Orion and the security it provided. They hadn't seen Kyle either. There was an underground parking lot below the building, but the vehicles had to exit on their side of the street. There was only one entry and exit, and in the hours they had been waiting, neither Steve nor Kyle had left the building.

Kyle thinks he's so tough but hides behind Orion. Although Onyx considered calling Kyle and challenging him to a duel, the thought made her laugh out loud.

"What?" asked Brain. "What's so funny?" he insisted.

"Your face is," Onyx replied, shifting in her seat. She was beginning to cramp up from sitting idly for so long.

"Fucking pussies," said Pinky, annoyed.

"All this power and shit, and they're afraid to come out to play," Onyx said and laughed.

"Look, it's Steve!" pointed out the brain seeing his car exit.

"Yeah, that's his car. Follow him," Onyx said excitedly.

Pinky immediately began to follow at a distance. "Hey, Brain, check our six. Make sure they're not using him as bait. I'll call the others and send my tracker location so they can meet us. We're going to need the reinforcements," Onyx told him.

There was another vehicle following Steve's car. Onyx knew this extra layer of security would complicate things, but she was determined. She was going to make a move. Kyle will know she is a ghost who can appear whenever she wants to disrupt his operations. She will call him once this is over to let him know he should thank her because Simon plans to replace him with Steve.

Since Simon had put Kyle in for "early retirement," Kyle will probably move first to eliminate Simon, and then Onyx will only have Kyle as a concern.

Steve arrived at his apartment, and Onyx jumped out of the car.

"Where are you going?" Brain asked her as she got out without consulting with them.

She was improvising but reconsidered going alone.

"You have your silencers, so let's go. You two take out the security. I'll take Steve. We can't let them go into the building. We need to surprise them in the parking lot. It's underground. Now, let's run in—move!" she ordered.

They exited the car, weapons in hand, and ran for the parking lot. Not a great plan, but sometimes, the best thing to do is the unexpected. People freeze when confronted with something they are not anticipating. No one likes the element of surprise, which is why people are so resistant to change.

What Onyx didn't know is that she was in for a colossal surprise herself. She underestimated Kyle once again. Perhaps the year away made her rusty.

Kyle knew Onyx was outside Orion and deliberately sent his best in Steve's car to trick her. His only regret is that he won't get to kill her himself. She was now no more significant than a measly, disgusting cockroach to him, a mere pawn in a chess game waiting to be stomped out. He was glad for her transgression. Were it not for what she did, Simon probably would've killed him long ago.

PART FOURTEEN

"We'll go to the hotel and get ready. The team is moving in on a target. We have orders to move in on them and extract—use force, if necessary," Ivan informed everyone.

Mateo looked at Ivan, but before he could speak, Ivan added, "nonlethal, of course."

Mateo rolled his eyes. *Something is off about this. The only people Onyx knows are Ivan and me*, he thought, staring at Ivan.

If any of the others attempt to engage her, she will think they are Orion, and she will shoot to kill, and I know none of these assholes will let her kill them, he told himself, feeling anxious.

This extraction was either a suicide mission or a hit, none of which Mateo signed up for when he agreed to it.

"You know she doesn't know we're coming, right? She doesn't know any of these people either," Mateo said, pointing at the rest of the team.

Ivan gave him a confused look, unsure of what Mateo meant.

"So, what leads you to believe she won't think we are Orion and fucking kill us all?" Mateo asked him, frustrated.

Max, the woman on the team, turned to face Mateo. "I don't know who you think your little girlfriend is, but if anyone dies tonight, it's her. She's not the only badass in town. She can come willingly, or I'll drag her," she warned Mateo.

Mateo laughed. "OK, tough shit. Good luck with that," he told her.

Ivan interjected, "Let's try to expedite this so that we can get back. I hate this city. I visited a few times and made it a point to not return since, so I want to leave as soon as possible," he said nervously.

"This jungle is for the strong. It chews and spits out the weak," Mateo said brusquely.

He and Ivan met at basic training. Although Ivan was born and raised in Florida and was not a fan of New York City, he did come up to visit Mateo once.

"What's the plan?" Max asked Ivan. "Are we just going to ambush them? As much as I don't want to agree with Mateo, I don't think that is a tactically sound approach. They should know we're coming," she stressed.

Ivan raised his hands in the air. "Look, I'm not calling the shots here. I'm just relying on the message," he admitted.

Max looked as if she were disgusted by this revelation. No one likes a weak or unassertive leader. People want a leader who will exude and inspire confidence. "All right, mouthpiece, how about you let me speak to the boss because *we* are the ones out here. *We* should be calling the shots, and quite frankly, you're useless," she stated, frustrated.

Ivan got in her face. "*I'm* calling the shots. We do as *I* say. If you don't like it, you can wait in the hotel. Anyone else who has a problem can also wait in the hotel. Do I make myself fucking clear?" he shouted.

Max snickered. "Oh, you *do* have it in you. Well, I like this guy a whole lot better now. The pussy was getting on my nerves, but we are still not going to surprise that fucking team and get killed, so I hope you have a fantastic fucking idea," she retorted.

Well, that's comforting, Mateo said to himself. *If we don't get killed by Onyx and her team, we'll end up killing each other*, he thought.

"Isn't Josh here with the chick?" Mateo overheard one guy whisper to Max.

"Yeah," she whispered back.

"I'm going to send him a message. I'll let him know we're coming," he said.

"Good shit. This clown is clueless. They should've left him in the office," Max said, staring at the back of Ivan's head, who was on the phone.

Our choices will haunt us for the rest of our lives … for better or worse.

They arrived at the hotel, and the room had everything they needed: weapons, ammunition, and medical kits. Everything was there, and they even had tactical clothing in everyone's size.

Mateo wanted to ask the guy who told Max that he would alert the person Josh on Onyx's team if he had received word, but he decided against it. He wasn't sure who he could trust or if there was a mission within this mission. He contemplated ditching them. He had a few buddies left here in New York. Some were in favor of the separation, while others were against it. Mateo was indifferent. All he wanted was to be left alone, and leaving would burn the bridge that leads back to Eden.

"Let's move!" Ivan yelled.

He had some newfound courage after his exchange with Max. All it takes is for a woman to challenge a man, so he can start acting like one.

Mateo laughed out loud at the thought. "Something funny, princess?" Max asked him.

"Yes, actually, there is. All it took was for you to call Ivan out, and he found his balls. He must've had them in his pocket the whole time," Mateo joked.

They both laughed at that. Mateo decided to turn on his charm. If he was going into a gunfight, he needed someone to have his back, and he put his money on Max.

The tactical van was big enough to accommodate all of them. So they quickly got in and drove off.

City traffic was no longer an issue; most people used mass transit. Gasoline prices had increased exponentially after the war. Gas was now a whopping hundred dollars a gallon.

Electric cars were not as convenient as people tried to persuade others to believe. Not only were charge stations few nor as readily available as gas stations, but the cost of electricity had quadrupled, so people stopped driving altogether.

The poor, whose numbers increased exponentially, added the middle class to its ranks, and they don't own vehicles. If they do have one, they rarely use it.

A fucking shit show this city now is. But as with everything else, people object at first and then conform. They stopped caring. They are getting free board, free internet, free food, and a universal check to live their life packed like sardines, in shoe box-size apartments, in government-run green zones. The Utopia everyone dreamed of … equity for all … or so we thought, Mateo mused, looking out the van window.

The 1 percent was still the 1 percent who had a massive transfer of wealth during the pandemic, making themselves even more ludicrously wealthy. Welcome to 2030!

Onyx, Pinky, and Brain arrived in the parking lot as Steve's security was exiting his vehicle, and Onyx took a shot right to the head.

The unknown man fell to the ground, and she felt a jolt of energy shoot up her spine. Pinky and the brain were exchanging gunfire with the security team following Steve.

They were ducking behind cars. "Go! Get the car; move. I'll cover!" Onyx yelled to Pinky, who ran out to the street level.

Suddenly, there were more people than Onyx expected—and no Steve. *It's a setup*, she thought, ducking.

The brain stayed with Onyx. They were shooting and retreating, and Onyx was pleased that he was anticipating her moves and followed her lead.

Not such a moron, after all, she thought.

Pinky arrived with the car. "Get in!"

The brain yelled. "I'll cover you," he told Onyx. She promptly ran to the vehicle, jumping into the passenger seat.

Onyx covered the brain and yelled for him to get into the car as she was shooting, but he was shot in the head before he could make it in the vehicle.

"Fuck! Go go go!" she shouted at Pinky, who was already reversing out of the lot as the security team was advancing.

Pinky peeled out and took off. Then they sat in silence for a long time.

"Shit, Josh should not have gone out like that. We were so close. Maybe if he had ducked instead of—" Onyx interrupted him.

"Don't do that; don't Monday morning quarterback. He did good, did his best, and died a hero in my eyes. A real gentleman. That was my fault. I should've covered him better. I have more experience," she told him.

They didn't say anything else after that.

They checked into a motel in the Bronx. Now, they had to change things up. They had become complacent, and now, Kyle was going to widen his search net.

Once in the room, Onyx went into the shower. Water had a soothing effect on her, and she wanted to think. She sent Jones a message that she was set up but refused to return. Now, she was angry and wanted to go after Kyle.

The three others with her had also arrived at the motel. "You should've waited for us," one of them told her.

"I saw an opportunity and had to take it," she replied. Then she told them to get some rest and that they would talk more in the morning.

"Where's Josh?" one of the other three asked Pinky.

"He's dead," Pinky replied bleakly.

"Did he have anything on him, any phone, identification?" another one asked.

"No. Onyx told us to leave everything in the car. If we didn't make it back, a cleanup team would find the car and take care of it," Pinky said.

Josh never received the message, so Onyx still didn't know that Ivan and Mateo were there.

"Pull over," Ivan instructed the driver of their van.

"We're going back to the hotel," he told them.

Everyone grumbled in protest. "What happened?" Mateo asked.

"They don't need us," Ivan said shortly.

"What happened to 'extract by force, if necessary'? Shouldn't we be going to their rendezvous and dragging them back with us?" Mateo challenged, and Ivan appeared annoyed.

"Yes, exactly! That's what we are doing. I am only awaiting a location as we speak," Ivan told him.

They went back to the hotel and ordered room service.

Mateo was getting anxious again. He didn't want to eat. He only desired to get Onyx, hop on the plane, and leave.

"Always some goddamn runaround," Mateo murmured under his breath.

Max, who was standing next to him, nodded. "What's so special about this chick anyway?" she asked.

Mateo pondered her question. What makes people unique? Is it their appearance? Their body? Their intellect? What is it that makes Onyx special?

It's difficult to explain, and the truth is that Onyx was extraordinary. She was magnetic, a vortex that attracted and pulled people in.

She was beautiful, charming, funny, intelligent, and had a glorious body, but so do many others. However, they are not, by any standard, unique, memorable, or unforgettable, but Onyx was. Why?

What was it that made her so irresistible and attractive?

"She knows who she is. She knows what she wants and is confident," he said, having left so much out.

If you pay attention, you will notice that some talented artists are unpopular, which applies to any art ... singing, acting, anything. But conversely, some people don't even have a single skill and are wildly famous. For the latter, their existence alone is a marvel. People are attracted to them, like moths to the light, because of their alignment with their authentic selves. They are what they want to be, unapologetically.

Everyone craves that freedom. All want that power. It is power, indeed. Still, most cannot even decide what to eat or wear, let alone know who they are. So they are content with mere existence, living vicariously through others, and obsessing with their courage of having figured it out.

"There has got to be more to it because all this fucking trouble for one little girl," Max insisted.

Mateo smiled. "There is infinite, a lot more to Onyx Pion than meets the eyes," he told her.

She elbowed him. "You love her?" she asked.

Ivan walked back into the room. He had stepped out to make a call. "OK, people, let's go. This is it; they're in a motel in the Bronx. Let's grab and go. Anything you don't want to take back, leave here. The cleanup crew will take care of it," he said.

They had allies on this side, spies, and Jones would have them remove any trace that anyone associated with the Florida Guard had been there.

PART FIFTEEN

The others were still in the room talking with Pinky, and Onyx wanted to be alone, so she went to the car to retrieve Josh's wallet and phone.

She sat in the car a long time, going through the few personal effects he had … debit cards, identification, and other miscellaneous business cards. She took one from a tattoo shop and put it in her pocket. Maybe she would get some ink when she got back. Surprisingly, she didn't have any.

His phone was locked. The background photo was the Punisher logo, the original one. She wondered if there was a special someone in his life and if he would be missed. What about his parents? Did he have a sibling? What had life been like for him?

Having been consumed with her need for vengeance, she never thought to ask.

It's sad, but people only wonder about others around them once they are gone. And unfortunately, most people don't appreciate them while they have them.

The truth is, they don't give those around them any attention unless they are behind a screen. She had only recently met Josh, and under the circumstances, that's the best they could've done to get acquainted, but his death put her other relationships into perspective.

For example, Mateo left, and not once did she reach out to him, not even to properly thank him. They had a long history; yet she treated him as if he were just some colleague of little importance. Like she never cared about him even a little.

A van pulled into the motel parking lot, and her skin bristled. Luckily, the engine was running. Pinky parked it near the exit. She had been listening to music and immediately turned off the radio.

The lot is where the entry is on one side, and you must go across the lot to exit. So she switched the car gear to drive, sinking into her seat.

Kyle must have tracked them there. Orion had cameras on that building that stretched city blocks. They must have gotten the plate and used the traffic cameras network to narrow their location.

"Fuck," Onyx said, pulling out slowly, with the lights off.

In survival situations, it's every person for themselves.

"Max, go in and get a room, and while you're at it, be persuasive in getting the room numbers we need. We'll be out here looking out," Ivan instructed.

Max opened the van door to get out. "I'll go with her," Mateo said, following.

"He sent me alone for a reason; my persuasion is not for those with a sensitive stomach," she said once they were out and she had shut the van door.

Mateo shook his head and kept silent. Finally, they walked in, and Max took out a paper with an array of photographs.

"Any of these people book a room?" she asked, showing it to the clerk.

He looked at them suspiciously. "I can't disclose that information," he replied.

Before Max could react, Mateo opened his wallet and quickly closed it again. "We are federal agents investigating a sex-trafficking ring. If you refuse to cooperate, we will charge you with conspiracy and obstruction of justice," he informed the clerk.

Hotels and motels were practically nonexistent; only a few remained because the oldest occupation in human history still existed. Many of the clients were in positions of power, so they decided to leave a few operational.

The clerk stared at Mateo, alarmed, and asked Max to see the photos again. "Yeah, three of those guys are here in separate rooms," he said, handing her back the paper.

"Of course, that's because they're hiding the victims in the rooms. Write down the room numbers and give them to my partner," Mateo ordered.

The clerk did as he requested. Mateo told him that they had alerted the local police and had a backup van outside but that he was to remain inside for his safety, even if he heard shooting.

"No need to alert the police because they are already on their way. These are dangerous people," Mateo said as he and Max walked out.

"Will you look at that? My man has a silver tongue. Nice job, princess," Max told him.

Mateo shook his head. "Come on, I want to get this shit over with," he said as they walked back to the others.

Onyx was doing her breathing exercises to keep calm. *They must all be dead by now.* She needed to ditch the car.

"Shit shit shit!" she said, hitting the steering wheel. She had left her phone charging in the room. So all she had was Josh's phone, which was locked and about to die. At least she had his cards since her wallet was also in the room.

No big deal, she thought.

It was almost two a.m. Car rentals were closed, and stealing cars was nearly impossible unless the vehicles were about two decades old.

After driving a few miles, she saw a bar. She parked the car and looked in the mirror, unable to recognize her reflection. She attempted to fix her curly hair. It was sticking up. "Damn, girl," she said to someone she didn't know. "You look rough. Let's see if you can work some magic."

The bar was nearly empty, with music playing low. *This place is a real shit hole*, she thought, surprised it was still open.

She saw two guys at the bar and walked over. "Is this stool taken?" she asked one of them.

"No, ma, you can sit," he said to her.

Onyx smiled at him. "Thanks, handsome," she said. She sat facing the man and played with her hair. She didn't lie. He *was* handsome, and she immediately thought of Jones, how she missed him and felt silly for not having left sooner.

The bartender came over. "What can I get you, gorgeous?" he asked Onyx.

"I'll have what he's having," she said, pointing at the guy next to her.

"It's on me," he said, inching closer to her.

"Thanks," she said, touching his arm.

"I'm Pablo," he said, extending his hand.

"Onyx," she said, holding it longer than necessary. "You have soft hands and a nice smile, Pablo," Onyx said.

"Thank you, gorgeous. It's nice to meet you. That's a nice name, by the way. Onyx, like the stone?" he asked, and she smiled.

"Thank you, yes. Exactly like the stone."

The bartender brought her a drink, gin and tonic. "Cheers!" she said, raising her glass to his.

Pablo was intrigued by this beautiful mystery woman and found it odd that she had come to the bar so later, so he said, "You're coming in here rather late, aren't you?" he added.

"Oh, I just finished my shift. I'm a nurse, and I'm off tomorrow," she said, drinking the glass's contents in one gulp. "It was a rough day. One of my patients passed away," she told him, eyes tearing.

"Oh, wow," Pablo said, surprised.

"He was young, so sad," she continued, dabbing her eyes.

Pablo placed a hand on her shoulder. "I'm sorry to hear that. That's terrible. Not an easy job you have. Thank you for what you do," he said, rubbing her back.

Onyx wanted to break his arm, but she smiled at him instead. "It's good to know that there are still kind people left in the world. You're handsome *and* sweet," she replied.

He beamed, and they continued to drink and talk.

"You live around here?" she asked casually.

"Yes, I do. About two blocks away. You want to get out of here?" he asked hopefully.

"Absolutely!" she exclaimed.

They left the bar and walked two blocks to his apartment building.

"What do you do?" she asked as they walked. It was cold, and she had forgotten her jacket. Pablo noticed Onyx was shivering and gave her his coat.

"I'm a train conductor for the MTA," he said proudly.

Onyx gasped with amazement. "Wow, that is *so* cool!" she answered.

He laughed. "I'm glad *someone* thinks so. It's a job that pays the bills and keeps me out of the green zone. I also do security on the side," he said, and Onyx tensed up.

"For whom?" she asked, hoping he didn't say, Orion.

"Alpha Security," he said, and Onyx sighed with relief.

Fortunately, Alpha is a mediocre security company that provides its personnel with inadequate training.

She held his hand. "Well, you're a superhero to me. Trains are cool, and so are you," she said, smiling.

They arrived at the apartment building, and Onyx looked around for cameras, fire escapes, and secondary exits, strategizing an alternate plan.

"Do you have a car?" she asked as he opened his apartment door.

"Yes, I barely drive it, but I have one. Don't worry, though. I'll take you home ... eventually," he grinned and shut the door.

"What the fuck do you mean she's not here?!" Ivan roared; he was furious.

He went to one room at a time. This team knew him personally. They had volunteered to come with Onyx. Ivan had handpicked them and knocked, hoping they'd recognize him and let him in without resistance.

They did, but Onyx was not there, and her belongings were still in her room. Pinky ran to the parking lot and confirmed that the car was gone.

"Maybe she went to get something to eat," he said, scratching his head.

Mateo sat on the edge of a bed and covered his face with his palms. *This cannot be real. It must be a dream.* Onyx went missing when Mateo thought it was over.

Where are you? What happened? he wondered. He sat on her bed, going through every possible scenario.

When the van pulled into the lot, he saw a car leave on the other side, but it was too far and dark for him to see the occupants. Onyx was very cautious. What if she thought Orion had found them and taken off?

He stood up. "Where was your vehicle parked?" he asked Pinky.

"Over on the other end, by the exit. She always likes to be near the exit," he explained.

Mateo nodded. "She saw the van and felt threatened. So, she's gone," he said.

Max was aggravated. "Gone where?"

Ivan punched the wall.

"I don't know. Onyx could be anywhere. Maybe she went after Kyle for sending a hit squad after her. Who knows with Onyx," Mateo said, sitting again. He was trying to think of places she would go and kept returning to himself. He was all she had; to her, he was in Florida.

"What would she do? What *could* she do? There was that lady from the church. What was her name? Alma!" he recalled.

Onyx would not put her in harm's way. He knew she was fond of Alma, and when she came to him initially, Onyx had stated that she had given Alma a copy of the file but felt remorseful that she had involved her in this and would not do it again, so he was out of ideas.

With no means of communication, her options were limited. No one commits numbers to memory anymore. Smart devices do all the work. So, finding Onyx would be like finding a needle in a haystack.

Ivan was on the phone with General Jones, who was livid.

Jones told Ivan that she knew about the chartered plane and its location and was probably on her way there and that he should assemble all personnel and go there for immediate departure.

If she was not there, he was to abort the mission. Jones had already misused too many resources and workforce on Onyx. She was on her own now.

Mateo was anxious. *What is Jones going to do now?* he wondered, and then Ivan returned.

"Alright, people, pack it up. The cleanup crew will be here in ten minutes, and we need to be gone," he said.

"Where are we going?" questioned Mateo.

"Back to Florida!" Ivan exclaimed, delighted.

Everyone else seemed glad about the news, but Mateo's heart sank. He hoped that Onyx would be headed back with them, but he also knew that Jones would not go the extra mile. All this was the best he could do, and it was more than Mateo could have imagined.

Onyx made a choice. She wanted to come back and get revenge for something that was her fault all along, and now she would be left alone to figure it out.

"You going to be, OK?" Max asked as she approached Mateo.

"She made her bed," Mateo said, taking her wallet from the nightstand.

"I guess, but I believe in no man left behind. So if you are cooking something up, count me in," Max said quietly.

Mateo looked at her with appreciation. "Thank you, but there isn't much we can do. I'm the one person she would try to contact, and she doesn't know I'm here," he confessed.

She slapped him on the back. "I'll be in the van. It's too fucking crowded here, and it smells like sweaty balls," she said.

Mateo laughed and followed her out. He also needed some air.

When Mateo and Onyx met, she was an empty canvas. Her life had not been easy. She had wounds more profound than the ocean and scars wider than the galaxy, but he felt in his heart that if she had allowed people in, maybe things would have turned out differently for her.

Sometimes people guard themselves to prevent further pain and go down a path of self-destruction, unable to heal and grow. Mateo tried hard to reach her during the months they spent together before she left for basic but was unsuccessful.

When she had military leave, she would come back to visit Mateo. However, there was no one else. Most of her family were in a different country, and she did not want to find or reconnect with them.

When Onyx left the service, she spent about a year with Mateo doing different security jobs until she landed the gig with Orion and was on her own. The job was consuming, and she drifted away. Onyx breathed and lived work. It's all she did.

Mateo had no way of finding her now. She always found him, and despite all that had happened, he wanted her to return safely to Florida and to the happy life she had built there with Jones.

"I have to say you are gorgeous. Your skin is flawless. I love it. It's dark and smooth like an onyx stone, and you have a banging body. Damn, girl, you're perfect," Pablo said, caressing her cheek.

She smiled and kissed his cheek. "Thank you," she said, looking into his eyes.

"You want something to drink, beautiful?" he asked.

"Water, please," she said, looking around. The green zone residents have a curfew. All must be in by midnight.

Only people with specific designations did not have to adhere to a curfew. Naturally, you must keep the workforce happy if you want this to work. Everyone did seem happy. Maybe Mateo was right. They want this, the National Guard patrols the streets, enforce the curfew, and everyone seems content.

Many working people choose to live in green zones to help combat climate change. But unfortunately, they don't get free room and board. They pay a fee, which is less expensive than rent at a privately owned building, most of which companies like FaceTome, Froogle, Jungle, Chirp, Space Linkage, Orion, Pharma Corp, and the Doors Foundation own.

Most of the employees of these heavy hitters live on their properties. So, what was there to change? It doesn't matter if the foundation is a lie if people are happy … right? People prefer comfortable lies to inconvenient truths.

"Here you go." Pablo handed her a glass of water. She took it, thanking him.

They sat at a dining table, and Onyx asked him about his family. He said his parents and siblings lived in the green zone, and he didn't see them often.

"Why?" Onyx asked, curious.

"That's just the way it is. I'm busy with work, most of my friends live out here, and I don't have the time," he admitted.

She nodded.

"I'll get us some beers," Pablo said.

When he walked to the kitchen, she retrieved the revolver she found in the abandoned building from her ankle holster.

Onyx kept it for luck. When they arrived in Florida, they took it, and she had asked Jones if she could have it back, and he promised he would try to locate it and return it to her. Sensing the weapon was of emotional value to Onyx, Jones placed it in a gift box and gave it to her. He had never seen her so excited about anything, and she rewarded him with incredible sex that night.

When Pablo returned, Onyx was holding the gun on the table. Shocked by the sight of the weapon, he dropped a bottle.

"It's OK," she reassured him.

Pablo stared at Onyx, paralyzed with fear.

"I'm not going to kill you unless you make me. Sit down, please," she said.

Shaking, he took a seat.

"I want to say thank you, I mean it, for your kindness and hospitality. Under different circumstances, I would have loved to get to know you better," she said, kissing him on the lips.

"Now, can you fetch your car keys, please? You have a beautiful home, by the way," Onyx admired.

Nervously, he stood and went to a keyholder hanging by the kitchen counter. He removed a set of keys and handed them to her.

"Thank you. I also need your phone and debit card, please," Onyx requested.

Pablo reached into his pocket and handed her the wallet and phone.

"No, I just want the debit card, not the whole wallet, and what is the unlock passcode for the phone?" she asked politely.

With trembling hands, he removed a debit card from the wallet and gave it to her with the phone.

"The code is 9999," he said, terrified.

"I appreciate it, Pablo. I meant what I said. You are sweet and handsome, and as much as I'd love to be having hot, steamy sex with you, I have to go because, unfortunately, people are trying to kill me, so please accept my sincerest apologies," she told him.

He nodded. "It's OK. I understand," he muffled out.

"Good, because now, I must restrain you. Remove the laces from your boots quickly, please. I'm a bit behind schedule," Onyx ordered.

He sat and removed the laces as requested, and she instructed him to go to his bedroom. "If you have to pee, I suggest you go now. We did drink a lot," she suggested.

He shook his head and continued to the bedroom. Onyx tied his wrists to the bed frame using the laces, and with the sheet, she tied his ankles in square knots, kissed him goodbye, and left.

PART SIXTEEN

General Jones informed Ivan that departure would not be until six that morning. They had no authorization to take off sooner, and no one had seen or heard from Onyx.

"Listen up. We can't leave until 0600 hours. So, if you want to get some shut-eye for a few hours, go ahead, but no one leaves for any reason," Ivan said, looking at Mateo.

Ivan had called Max and Mateo back in. They had been waiting in the van, and he was concerned that those two would take off searching for Onyx. He already had enough problems. They would hunker down in the motel until it was time to go, which was not long. It was already about three thirty in the morning, and they would leave in another hour.

This Onyx situation was a never-ending nightmare for Mateo. The more desperate he was to return to Florida, the longer it was postponed. Would he *ever* wake up from this dream? He felt trapped in an Onyx loop. He could not escape her. All the memories with her flashed in his mind's eye like a movie.

No one slept. Everyone was anxious to leave. Mateo thought about all the things Onyx could be doing now, and the outcome was always negative in all those scenarios.

Ivan said Onyx wasn't at the airport, and no one had seen her there, but she knew about it. So, maybe she was still finding her way over there. It was a long distance from the motel, and knowing her, if she thought Kyle tracked her here, she would ditch that car. But Mateo still had hope, and maybe this delay was a good sign. It was a way of giving her a chance to escape with the rest of them.

He was in the room with Max and Pinky. "That's what she called me," Pinky told Mateo when he introduced himself, and Mateo asked if that was his real name.

Pinky was snoring, and Max and Mateo exchanged looks. "At least someone is getting his beauty sleep," she whispered.

"I wish I could nap, but my anxiety is at one hundred right now," Mateo confessed, and Max laughed.

"Relax. We are almost out of here, I know you wanted her to be with us, but trust that she will find her way," Max told him.

Mateo closed his eyes. It was almost serendipitous how people unconsciously say things that are synchronicities. Her telling him to trust that Onyx will find her way was a divine message.

Orion agents were following Onyx and shooting at her. She felt blood but didn't know where it was coming from. She was hit again in the head, and Mateo woke up panting.

It feels so real, he thought, realizing that Pinky and Max were up and ready to go. "Good morning, sunshine. I'm glad you took that nap you craved, but it's time to go," Max said, leaving the room.

Mateo quickly got up, then rushed to get ready and convene with everyone outside. The cleanup crew was there with a second van to transport them to the airport.

They were leaving, and if Onyx didn't make it, they would go without her. Mateo feared he would never see her again. While in Florida, the notion of never seeing her again was acceptable because he knew she was content and safe.

That's what happens when you genuinely care about someone. It doesn't matter if the person is a part of your life. What matters is that they are well.

The car was nice, relatively new, and immaculately clean, like his apartment. Pablo is a nice guy. Maybe in another life ... Onyx thought.

It was nice to pretend like she was normal for a few hours and have a decent conversation, but the reality is that she had no idea what she was going to do now.

Onyx couldn't decide between going into Orion guns blazing or getting on that plane and going home to Jones. She feared that if she continued down this path, she would be like Icarus, flying too close to the sun.

She could go by Orion to see if she got lucky. Onyx felt like she had gone mad, like this thirst for revenge had taken control over her and did not allow her to reason. It was her ego. She could not stand the thought that Kyle had won, but what did he win? Wasn't she the one who escaped to paradise? Instead, he was still here, in this toxic city, crippled by anger and famished for power.

Sometimes you are the victors and don't even know it. So lost in comparison with others, you fail to see the truth instead of appreciating what you already have.

Onyx was outside Orion headquarters as if the car had gotten her there on autopilot. She parked the vehicle as a million thoughts raced through her mind. One would reason that going back to Florida was the obvious choice. Of course, there was nothing to contend with in Florida, and Onyx knew it, but the truth is, the human psyche is far more complex. In almost every situation, people know the best course of action, yet, they overanalyze a thing into its most intricate state, unleashing endless troubles for themselves.

In her case, Onyx had become fanatical, obsessed with her ideals, and unable to do what was truly best for her.

Frequently, individuals spend their time blaming external situations and people for the plights in their lives, incapable of taking responsibility that life had manifested out of their creation.

As Onyx reached to open the glove compartment to see if maybe Pablo had kept a gun, a bullet grazed her left ear, shattering the glass.

"Fuck, a sniper!" she shouted.

She stayed down and used the backup camera to get out of the parking spot. As soon as the car was in motion, bullets began to hail down, and she sped away.

Mateo and the crew were on their way to the airport, and he felt ill. His stomach was in knots, and he had an awful taste of vomit in his mouth.

The plane wasn't ready when they arrived. The maintenance crew was waiting for fuel to arrive. The craft was an older model, and Mateo found it funny how costly this expedition turned out to be for Jones … all because his favorite vice had run astray. He was trying to find humor in this ordeal to keep calm because he'd be home in a few hours, and Onyx would be lost to them forever.

Where is she? Is she alive? he wondered.

"If Onyx knows that there is a way out, wouldn't that be the obvious choice?" he asked himself, but with Onyx, nothing was simple. Onyx didn't understand simplicity. She liked complicated. Maybe it was a way to keep herself mentally stimulated. Those who deliberately made their lives difficult may do it because they are addicted to the thrill.

Her defiance wasn't about her changing anything. It was about giving her life some meaning and purpose, even negatively. Onyx didn't have family, friends, or anything seemingly meaningful to live for, so she had to construct situations that gave her that meaning and sense of importance. She didn't know that living is of tremendous value and that the choices you make with the opportunity to be alive are what matter.

Jones must be of little importance to her or cannot satisfy this need because why would she not find a sense of urgency in getting back to her life with him?

The crew members didn't have much to load and asked them to board the plane while waiting for the fuel. They had snacks, and Max inquired if there were any alcoholic beverages. "It's five o'clock somewhere, and this trip was stupid," she laughed.

Mateo unconsciously tapped his knee as he shook his leg up and down. He felt uneasy. His stomach was fluttering with anxiety.

"We are here, princess, on the plane. Calm down. You're making me nervous," Max stated, rolling her eyes.

Ivan was texting, probably giving Jones a play-by-play, Mateo assumed.

The fuel truck was there. "Finally!" Ivan exclaimed. "I can't wait to be up in the air," he said.

There was palpable tension in the air. Everyone was on edge, anxious to take off. A crew member gave beer to all who wanted some, but Mateo shook his head when she offered him one.

"Got any coffee?" he asked. He had not been able to sleep more than a few minutes, and this ordeal had taken its toll. He felt exhausted.

"A few more minutes to take off. Make yourselves comfortable," the pilot said as he entered the cockpit.

Onyx felt blood dripping down her neck from the bullet that grazed her ear. She saw two vehicles following her. Although she was moving fast, they were close behind.

This isn't good, she thought, and then bullets shattered the rear windshield.

"Shit!" she screamed and swerved in and out of traffic lanes to avoid direct fire.

Onyx had to get out, and she decided to head for the airport where Jones had a chartered plane. Maybe it was still there. But unfortunately, no one could've shown up if they were all dead.

Onyx's only shot of survival was to get out of New York; right now, the only option was that plane.

One of the vehicles following her was now beside her passenger side. The driver rammed into the side of her car, and the side mirror flew off. She had hoped to leave Pablo's car intact. "There goes that," she said, speeding up and shooting at the driver.

The second vehicle approached her on the driver's side, and she pushed the gas pedal to the floor. She couldn't let them sandwich her in because a third vehicle had now joined the party.

She could not help but see images of her life flash in her mind. What a great machine the brain is, powered by human consciousness. She was under extreme pressure and stress, but somehow, her mind engaged her with her memory, and as she analyzed those images, she realized that if this were the end, it would be a waste.

Onyx had not lived the life she truly wanted. There was still far too much she had not done or experienced. She didn't want her story to end this way because it would be incomplete. How many people live unsatisfied, unfulfilled, unhappy, and miserable with the life they've chosen, in complete denial, trying to convince themselves of the contrary ... unsuccessfully.

Onyx had never been happy. She was always looking for ways to distract herself from her traumas and pain, like everyone else, but not everyone managed to place themselves in life-and-death situations. Therefore, they lacked such extreme contemplative opportunities.

Onyx felt misunderstood. People judge you by the lens of others, and human emotions distort that. As a result, people's perception of you is usually inaccurate, compounded by what they would like you to be or who they think you are. It is, however, of no significance because you never truly know a person.

What you think of yourselves is the only thing that matters because most people see in others a projection of themselves, whether they like it or not. People are loved today and hated tomorrow, and none of it has anything to do with them.

Everyone is responding to life from the filter of their perception, and the only thing you can do is be who you, indeed, are.

Onyx continued to shoot as she drove, going as fast as possible on the highway. Her pursuers were close behind, and she had to shake them off. It would be impossible to board a plane taking heavy fire, but this was her only option.

She slammed on the brakes and turned the car around, speeding back off the exit. She would get on the expressway again at another entrance.

Her tactic paid off because she managed to lose those tails, but she wasn't too excited because she knew they'd call it in, and there will be five new cars filled with shooters shortly. So she was only trying to buy herself a little time.

She was getting on that plane—on any aircraft—even if she had to fly it herself.

Onyx got on the highway again, and already three vehicles were chasing her. "Fuck!" she yelled, shooting at her new pursuers.

She exchanged fire continuously with those chasing her now. Finally, one vehicle crashed into the median. She must have hit her target and felt a boost of confidence, but there were still two other vehicles in hot pursuit.

Meanwhile, the airplane was fueled and ready to go. The crew was preparing to close the door when there was a loud noise outside.

Mateo saw through the airplane window that a vehicle had smashed the gate and was speeding down the runway, with two others chasing close behind, but the gunshots got everyone's attention.

"What the fuck?" Mateo said.

The occupants of the vehicles were in a fierce gunfight. "You have to be fucking kidding me!" Max exclaimed, coming across the aisle to Mateo's side for a better look.

"It's Onyx!" exclaimed Mateo, jumping out of his seat.

The rest were looking out of the windows, and Ivan's face was pale with shock.

"We need to help her. Are there any weapons?" Mateo asked, looking at Ivan.

"Of course," Ivan said nervously, pulling a duffel bag from under his seat. He opened it and handed everyone a weapon. Max pulled one out from her ankle holster.

"You assholes really gave up your guns?" she asked, walking toward the exit, taking another gun as she disembarked.

Mateo was already outside. He ran over and stood behind the SUV still parked there, taking a shot at the vehicle to Onyx's left. He aimed at the front tire.

They were approaching at high speeds and still a significant distance away. "Relax. Wait for them to get closer," Max told him as she came behind him and placed her hand on his shoulder.

"I have your six; be patient. We'll get your girl home as fate should have it," she said, and Mateo nodded.

Mateo had his sights fixed on the vehicles. If that were Onyx, he would ensure she boarded that damn airplane.

The others positioned themselves near the plane with weapons ready, and as soon as the vehicles approached, they opened fire, bringing the pursuing cars to a stop.

They remained on the runway at a distance, and Onyx knew it was a matter of time before that place was swarming with more vehicles, so they had to leave immediately.

Onyx pulled over in front of the SUV and exited her vehicle, weapon ready.

"Onyx!" Mateo called out to her. "Onyx, it's me, Mateo," he said, remaining behind cover for fear she would shoot him.

"Mat!" she screamed and ran to where he and Max were standing.

She hurled her body onto his in a tight embrace. "What are you doing here?" she asked, surprised.

"What does it look like he's doing? He came to save your ass, you brat!" Max said, keeping an eye on the now-stopped vehicles.

"Friend of yours?" Onyx asked Mateo, who nodded.

"Charming," she said facetiously, "but we have to get the fuck out of here. Fast, before they call in more firepower," Onyx warned.

Max elbowed Mateo. "She's right. Let's get the fuck out of here," Max insisted.

Mateo aimed down the runway to where the vehicles were stationary. "Take her. I'll cover," he said to Max.

"Like hell, you will!" Onyx said stubbornly, but Max was already pulling her arm.

"Look, sunshine, you've already caused enough trouble. You're getting on that plane, or I'll drag you. The princess will be fine. Let's go," Max told her.

Max and Onyx ran across the tarmac, and as they did, the vehicles moved and began to fire. Mateo and the other engaged as Max and Onyx boarded the aircraft.

Onyx felt as though she had an out-of-body experience. But then, things started to slow down as she and Max entered the plane.

Why is Mateo here? That was not part of the plan. He was supposed to be safe with his cult, in the swamp, peacefully living out the rest of his days, she thought.

Onyx had come to terms with that. She was happy for Mateo, and his being here was something she had not foreseen, making her completely uncomfortable.

Jones, she thought. *Why would he reach out to Mat? Why bring him out here? Why send all these people?* she wondered.

She had it. The plane was helpful enough. Her stomach turned, and there was a pain in her chest. "Let's go!" she shouted. "Get everyone in here," she said to Ivan as he boarded.

"They're coming. Relax. *You're* the one who arrived with unwanted guests. We have to mitigate this fucking situation before we can take off," Ivan told her angrily.

She rolled her eyes. "Well, I'm going back out there to help," she said, walking past him, and he quickly grabbed her arm.

"Sit the fuck down. You've caused enough trouble already!" he told her menacingly. Ivan was willing to shoot her in the leg. Now that she was here, she was definitely going back with him.

They glared at each other. "That's what I said, sunshine," Max added as she pushed them.

"I'll go," Max volunteered.

The others were already filing in. Mateo was engaged, and Max called to him. "I'll cover. Get the fuck over here so we can go home," she yelled.

Onyx was nervously looking out the window. Mateo was still not on board, and she was anxious about him. She didn't care about any of the others. All Onyx wanted was for Mateo to get on the fucking airplane. Pinky and he were the only two still left out there, and she was losing her mind. Only one shooter remained; she had exited the vehicle and was fiercely engaging.

I guess she's not going out without a fight, Onyx thought as she looked on.

Max was shooting from the stairs, and Mateo ran across. He was almost at the foot of the stairs when the cunt shot him.

Onyx cried out in agony. Time froze as she saw Mateo's body hit the runway.

She jumped over seats and out of the plane. The shooter got in her vehicle and reversed down the runway. Tempted to follow her, Onyx ran to Mateo instead.

"Mat!" she shrieked as she held him in her arms.

"It's OK, kid," he said smiling. "Don't worry about me. I'll be fine. Just get on that damn plane and go home," he told her.

Tears were streaming down her face and flowing onto his. "*We* are getting on that plane," she said, sobbing uncontrollably as blood pooled around him.

"Onyx," he said, squeezing her hand, "let all of this go. Please be happy. Try to find joy in life. Stop fighting. Promise me!" he begged, and she nodded, unable to speak.

She had a knot in her throat. Her tears burned as they gushed from her eyes, and her chest ached. The physical pain she experienced was devastating and paralyzing. Mateo shut his eyes … and died. Onyx screamed with despair and hugged him tightly against her body.

PART SEVENTEEN

Onyx arrived at the therapist's office, the dream still vivid in her memory. She could recall every detail. She felt it was significant and was not surprised she had this early appointment with Dr. Seeland.

Onyx did not believe that having such a dream the night before meeting with her was a coincidence. She was eager to discuss the dream with her therapist. Dr. Seeland always had something profound and insightful to say about anything Onyx went through, including her dreams.

She had strange dreams frequently, but they were worse now. Her anxiety and depression had also worsened. She was angry all the time and had difficulty managing her rage.

Onyx felt alone, with no one to talk to and no one who understood her. As a result, she had severe trust issues and difficulty connecting with others. Nothing new, but it's the first time she'd gotten help.

Most days, Onyx felt as if life had no meaning. She didn't enjoy being alive, and her thoughts often got dark, frightening her.

"Good morning, Onyx. Nice to see you again. How have you been?" the therapist asked with a pleasant smile. Onyx didn't like many people, but the doc had grown on her.

Dr. Seeland had a melodic voice, a strange accent Onyx did not recognize, and was attractive. She was a lovely older woman with white hair and pale skin. Her eyes reminded Onyx of the ocean, a deep shade of cobalt blue. Onyx enjoyed seeing her and interacting with her.

Onyx had been seeing Dr. Seeland for a few months, and she felt that talking to her was invaluable. *Maybe she thinks I'm completely crazy*, Onyx thought after their last visit. Onyx was fascinated by how professional and impartial the doc was as she listened to people's deepest, darkest thoughts, feelings, and desires.

What exciting stories she must know, and Onyx felt like that was something she could do … listen to others without judgment because she was not perfect and had made many mistakes.

People are here just trying to figure life out with no instruction manual. Of course, some are doing it more gracefully than others, but there was nothing wrong with admitting you need help and acknowledging you have difficulty coping. Sometimes, life gets complicated, and you lose hope, but you must carry on. You must persevere.

"I'm doing OK," Onyx said, sitting nervously and pushing some hair behind her ear.

Dr. Seeland sat across from her, notepad and pen in hand. Onyx wondered if she went home and read those notes to understand better or if she only did it to appear more engaged than she was. It gave her patients the illusion that she genuinely cared … or were they only a paycheck?

Onyx sensed Dr. Seeland cared deeply about helping her. She had learned to read people from a young age. It must have been the survival instinct. Growing up in foster care was challenging. She developed anxiety from a young age. Moving from home to home, constantly changing caregivers, and not knowing if they would harm her were nerve-racking.

So, she had to learn to read the adults. Children are naturally good at it, but when you grow up as Onyx did, you quickly become a master.

"Have you been sleeping better since our last meeting?" Dr. Seeland asked Onyx.

Dr. Seeland had suggested Onyx do breathing exercises before sleep and try to visualize herself floating into space, into a beam of light, where she became one with it. However, she still had difficulty falling asleep, and when she did sleep, she had awful nightmares.

Dr. Seeland also suggested she keep a sleep journal to help her remember and so that they can discuss the dreams in detail, something about her subconscious mind.

Today, Onyx did not need the journal. Instead, she clearly remembered the dream.

"Not really," she admitted, picking her fingernails.

"Are you still having bad dreams?" Dr. Seeland asked, and suddenly, Onyx felt sad and did not want to discuss the dream.

"Do you believe that dreams can predict the future?" Onyx asked her, disheartened.

"In dreaming, we access infinite space, where variant lifelines or timelines exist in consciousness but have not yet materialized. We manifest them based on choice. We decide which lifeline we physically want to create by our predominant thoughts and beliefs," she told Onyx.

Onyx looked confused, and Dr. Seeland smiled, aware she didn't answer her question.

"The future is not set in stone. There are infinite future possibilities, and we move into a specific one every time we make a decision," Dr. Seeland said.

Onyx considered what she had said. "What about when we dream of people we have never seen before?"

"We often dream of unfamiliar faces and places because we have yet to bring these alternate timelines into conscious reality; we never materialize some because dreams are a collection of data from the collective human consciousness," she said.

Most days, Onyx had no idea what Dr. Seeland meant. Unfortunately, today was one of those days; yet, she still enjoyed listening to her.

"Some of what you encounter in dreams may not be a product of your consciousness. We perceive time as linear, but all that is, was, and will exist simultaneously in the infinite space of multidimensionality. In dreaming, we're just accessing information," Dr. Seeland told her.

Onyx looked confused. "So, by that definition, we can theoretically peer into the future and meet people from our dreams in real life," Onyx said, and Dr. Seeland looked at her inquiringly.

"I believe we can. Although often, people will not look as they did in our dreams, we will recognize their essence. So, anything is possible," Dr. Seeland said.

Onyx continued to look down at her nails and bit her lip.

"Sweetheart, what is bothering you?" Dr. Seeland asked, concerned.

"I had this dream last night. It felt so real," Onyx began, finally making eye contact. She proceeded to go over the dream in detail. Toward the end, she burst into tears, and Dr. Seeland handed her a box of tissues.

"Go on," she encouraged.

"'Onyx,' he said, squeezing my hand, 'let all of this go. Please be happy. Try to find joy in life. Stop fighting. Promise me!'" Onyx recounted.

She was now sobbing in agony, and Dr. Seeland sat beside her and rubbed her back comfortingly.

"I nodded, unable to speak. I had a knot in my throat. My tears burned as they poured from my eyes, and my chest ached. The physical pain was like none I'd ever felt before. I still feel it now—and he died! I screamed and hugged him tightly. Blood was everywhere, and it hurt so bad," Onyx recalled painfully.

She turned and hugged her therapist. She was not one for hugging, but the pain was still there, tugging at her heartstrings, smothering her.

"Let it out, Onyx. Feel the pain. Don't suppress it. Feel it, then let it go," Dr. Seeland recommended.

Onyx composed herself and wiped her face, using tissue from the box Dr. Seeland had provided.

"Onyx, you are eighteen years old. It's 2020, not some distant, dark future. You've been through a lot. You will be graduating high school soon, and you fear the changes that come with that," Dr. Seeland reminded her.

Onyx nodded in agreement. "I was tough and confident in my dream. I wish I were that way now, and I don't know anyone named Mateo. How could I possibly feel devasted about someone who isn't real?" she asked, her eyes still wet.

"You can be anything you want. You just haven't decided who you are yet, and the mind makes it real. Just because it happened in a sleeping state doesn't mean it wasn't real. I believe that the man, Mateo, in your dream, is an aspect of your consciousness, a manifestation of your unconscious mind. A version of you that you wish you were, and the death of that aspect caused you great pain. Perhaps you feel you will never achieve that version of yourself. You dislike, as most people do, your perceived negative traits, and so you are angry all the time because you believe something is wrong with you, which, in some cases, leads to a distorted self-image or self-hatred," Dr. Seeland explained.

Onyx sat quietly, still thinking of the dream and everything the doctor said.

"Our internal struggle is never about others. It is always the I against me. We are our own worst enemies. Our ultimate goal is to conquer our negative low-vibrating subconscious, conditioned through many years of foreign ideas, beliefs, culture, religion, parents, family, friends, education, and everything else we have experienced since birth. But first, we must free ourselves, strip away all the things that are not our own, find our truth, create our unique dogma, and finally begin to be our true selves. Until then, we will struggle within ourselves," she told Onyx.

"I have no idea who I am. I feel lost and worthless. How could I possibly figure it out? But at least in my dream, I knew I was sure of myself," Onyx confessed.

"You must find coherence between heart and mind and manifest who you truly are. Emulate what you like about the Onyx of your dreams, but only if it rings true with who you desire to be," Dr. Seeland said.

"Do you think that will work? Figuring out who I am is the key?" Onyx asked.

"I know it. Then, and only then, will you find true peace and happiness. Life isn't about doing; it is simply being. The flower doesn't think or stress over blooming; yet it does. So do not allow your circumstances to dictate who you are. You are not what happened to you. You are who you want to be," she told her.

Onyx looked disappointed because she was still thinking of Mateo. She didn't want him to be a fragment of her subconscious mind. Instead, she wished he was real.

"What?" Dr. Seeland asked.

"I was hoping he was real and that he is out there somewhere," Onyx admitted.

The doctor laughed. "I can understand why he was remarkable, but guess what? You can manifest anything into physical reality. It may not be exact, the Mateo of your dreams, but someone similar … or *better*," the doctor promised her.

Onyx smiled; she liked the idea of that.

"You have your whole life ahead of you. So look forward with excitement, and think about all the wonderful things you have yet to experience and all the wonderful people you will meet," Dr. Seeland said.

Onyx thought about things she wanted to do, like dancing, prom, exotic vacations, bars, and hiking, and was saddened because she needed friends to do all those things.

She nodded and began to pick her fingernails again. "I don't know what I'm going to do. I'm no good with people, I have no friends, no one likes me, I don't like me … It's all so complicated," Onyx told her.

Dr. Seeland paused and allowed Onyx to sit with her emotions before continuing.

"You must be consciously aware of your thoughts and feelings. Accept who you are and extend all love to yourself first. Loving yourself is the key to happiness. So, Onyx, when you love and accept yourself, when you like yourself, others will too," Dr. Seeland assured her.

"It's hard," Onyx said.

"I know, but you must persist and never give up. That will be the most rewarding thing you'll ever do," Dr. Seeland reassured her.

Onyx nodded.

"We are evolving consciousness, and it is all about energy, vibration, and frequency. You must emit what you want out into the Universe. It is no easy task. It requires work, but I know you're tired of feeling sad, so why not try a new approach?" Dr. Seeland suggested.

"I'll do my best," Onyx promised, and then their time was up. She left Dr. Seeland's office, not necessarily feeling better.

Dr. Seeland never managed to help her feel better. That is why she kept seeing her; she may not feel better, but she better understood who she was.

People see a conventional therapist so they can put a Band-Aid over whatever they perceive as a problem with themselves or their lives. But although they may put all the advice into practice, there's always something missing, an unfillable void.

Onyx saw Dr. Seeland because her school counselor made her. She had gotten into fights at school, other work incidents, and at her latest home. So, naturally, the school counselor, attempting to keep her from getting into serious trouble, said Onyx had anger management issues.

When Onyx refused to see the school psychologist, she recommended Onyx to her friend, Dr. Seeland.

Despite her reservations about seeing a therapist, Onyx liked Dr. Seeland's unorthodox approach. It helped her understand and, most importantly, accept herself the way she was.

People live fervently trying to change everything, from themselves to those around them, and never take the time to understand and accept things exactly as they are. How simple would life be if you just chose to be what you are instead of desperately attempting to become something you are not.

Dr. Seeland was right. Onyx was tired of being a victim, constantly feeling sorry for herself, and being sad. There had to be more to life.

It was a sad dream, but she was fierce, resilient, and brave in it. It's possible that she can embody those traits, and if Mateo is a manifestation of her unconscious mind, she should display everything he was … optimistic, charming, kind, and selfless.

Dr. Seeland said it's a matter of choice, so I choose that, she thought, walking out of the office building.

She looked at the gas station across the street. Two dollars and thirty-nine cents read the sign. She smiled. She didn't drive, but she was glad it wasn't a hundred dollars.

It was a beautiful Saturday morning in May. Onyx will be graduating soon. Her eighteenth birthday was the previous month. She was now an adult, free to live as she pleased, and the notion of that made her happy. She wore a busted ThunderCats T-shirt, black sneakers from Five and Below, with raggedy jeans from the local thrift shop. Looking down at her outfit, she said, "I love it, and I love you, Onyx Pion!"

Onyx was thrilled to be an adult. Even though she didn't feel like one, she was happy she could leave the foster system.

She rented a room from an elderly couple who needed help paying their rent, which was what Onyx needed.

Onyx worked part time after school, and as soon as she graduated next month, she would begin work full time. She had been accepted to some local colleges, but attending would be challenging. She had to work full time to support herself, and college was not a viable option with no other support. So, now, she was considering the military.

They offered her an education, free room and board, and a ticket out of this city. Then, once her contract was up, she could get a job and find her place.

PART EIGHTEEN

On graduation day, Onyx wore blue jeans from the thrift shop, a black T-shirt, and her black sneakers. *The gown will cover it,* she thought. *It's not like anyone will be there to take pictures.*

She wanted this day to end. Initially, she wasn't going, but Dr. Seeland and her counselor insisted that she do.

"You need to show up for yourself, celebrate yourself, and rejoice in your accomplishments," her counselor told her when she expressed trepidation over it.

"I'll be there for you, Onyx," her counselor said, so finally, Onyx agreed to attend.

Fortunately, the ceremony was short, and to her surprise, Dr. Seeland was also in attendance.

"Congratulations, Onyx. I am extremely proud of you, I know you didn't want to be here, but you came. That was courageous of you. I want you to keep finding the courage to do the things that scare you," Dr. Seeland said.

Onyx smiled. Dr. Seeland and her counselor took her to a nice restaurant to eat, and Onyx was happy.

Everything is going to be all right, she thought.

"When do you start working full time?" Dr. Seeland asked.

"Tomorrow!" Onyx exclaimed excitedly.

"That soon? I thought you would want to relax a bit, maybe sight-see, go to the museums, Central Park, or something like that," Dr. Seeland said.

Onyx shook her head. "I love those things, but I can do them on my days off. Right now, I only want to focus on work," she said, eating fried shrimp.

Dr. Seeland wore a beige suit, and her counselor had on a floral blouse with black slacks. Onyx felt underdressed.

The restaurant was packed. Many other graduates looked good in their Sunday best as they took photos with their families.

Onyx decided she wouldn't feel sorry for herself. Instead, she was thankful that her counselor and the doc had made this kind gesture. She knew that it could be worse. She could be alone.

She smiled, thinking how it would sound if someone asked who the two ladies were. *Oh, just my shrink and counselor because I'm a complete nut job*, she thought.

"Oh, I was thinking about enlisting in the military," she added, and Dr. Seeland looked at her, concerned.

"That's a great idea!" her counselor exclaimed happily.

"That's new," Dr. Seeland said, reaching for her hand. "Is this about the dream?" she asked, squeezing it.

"In part," Onyx said, taking a bite from one of the fries on her plate.

"I see. Well, remember to make good choices," Dr. Seeland said, releasing her hand.

Onyx laughed. "Don't worry, Doc. The world can save itself. I have myself to worry about," she joked.

They all laughed and finished their meals, talking about Onyx and her future plans. Onyx informed Dr. Seeland that she probably would not see her as frequently and expressed her gratitude for coming out to support her.

"We will always be here for you," her counselor said when they had finished, and then they all went their separate ways.

Onyx dumped the cap and gown in the trash and went for a walk. She didn't like getting home too early. The elderly couple were lovely but liked to chat, and Onyx wasn't in the mood.

Her foster mother was a despicable drunk, and Onyx was glad to be rid of her. With the help of her counselor, Onyx reported her to ensure she was never allowed to foster children again. She probably would have never done that, but after a glimpse into a dream world where she was confident and stood up for something, Onyx decided to start with the little things, like reporting Ms. Vallejo.

Onyx walked around for hours, thinking about what the next chapter in her life would bring. She was excited about work the next day. She enjoyed going there because it was not a conventional job setting.

Onyx worked at a Jungle warehouse on Staten Island. It was quite the mission getting there. She had to take the train, the ferry, and then a bus, but she enjoyed the commute. It gave her something to distract herself.

Work did not require much human interaction. Everyone did their job and went home, and she loved it. She liked keeping busy without human contact. She worked the night shift, which was better for her. There were fewer people at work and during the commute.

That day after her shift, she went home, took a short nap, and got up to go for a run. Dr. Seeland had advised her to start an exercise routine to help with her depression … something about endorphins, dopamine, or whatever. But unfortunately, Onyx could not remember exactly.

Onyx laughed, thinking about it. She felt a lot happier being on her own. Independence felt good. It suited her. Maybe that's what she needed all along. And running was liberating. She liked it. There were many things she was discovering and enjoying.

"Try new things," her counselor suggested, so she did.

She started going to the movies alone. Dr. Seeland said you don't need to wait for people to come into your life to do things and enjoy them. "Once you begin to love life, people come," she had said. So, Onyx was going to do just that.

Often, people want to see a movie or go out to eat and don't because they have no one to accompany them, so what? Go on your own. Don't sit and watch life pass you by; make life *happen* as you go.

Onyx had never been to a movie theater and found it a wonderful experience. She never imagined that she would enjoy it all by herself.

Going down the stairs one morning, Onyx encountered a neighbor from the floor below as she came out of her apartment.

"Hi, going for a run?" the neighbor asked, and Onyx turned to look behind her, wondering if the question was directed to her because she still lacked confidence and a sense of worthiness. Onyx never expected people to speak to her.

"Oh, hi, yes, I am," she replied awkwardly.

"I'm new to the neighborhood. Just moved in with my mom, starting college in September, and I want to get in shape. I put on a few pounds during remote learning. I'll probably be doing remote this first semester too, but I don't want my ass to get any bigger. I've seen you running a few times. Can I join you?" she asked, and they both laughed.

That was a mouthful, Onyx thought. *Is that what regular people do? Do they tell their life story in one breath to strangers?*

Hi. I'm Onyx. I grew up in foster care because I'm an orphan. I suffer from anxiety and depression, and I hate people, she thought, smiling as they continued walking down the stairs.

"I'm Samantha, by the way," the talkative girl said. But my friends call me Sam.

Onyx gave her a closed-lipped smile.

"What's your name?" Sam asked, wrinkling her brows.

"Oh, I'm Onyx," she said quickly.

Onyx had many conversations in her head and often forgot she hadn't said them out loud, mainly because they were not always what was politically correct. Also, she liked to listen to other people speak. She hated talking about herself.

"Nice to meet you. That's a cool name," she said, and Onyx felt as if she had heard that before.

"Thanks," she mumbled as they got outside.

Onyx was not good at initiating or carrying on a conversation. She felt awkward talking to people and wouldn't be surprised if Sam thought she was weird and never spoke to her again.

However, over the next few months, Onyx was less depressed, and she and Sam hung out more. Sam had tons of friends, and Onyx met a lot of them. Unfortunately, they were all in college, and Onyx felt like the oddball but remembered what Dr. Seeland said: *"Don't worry about what other people are doing; don't compare yourself to others. Their experience is not your own, and vice versa."*

Onyx didn't care that she wasn't in college like they were. Instead, she felt relieved they all seemed stressed out about schoolwork.

Life cannot be one size fits all. Instead, it must be tailored to each individual to accommodate their uniqueness. So, Onyx was more comfortable with being herself and doing things differently these days.

Dr. Seeland also said, "People don't care or think about the next person with the frequency we believe. People are also generally consumed with themselves, worried about their own trivialities."

Onyx now felt less anxious. Having friends was excellent. However, she still enjoyed doing things herself, like going to the movies and museums.

On her days off, Onyx went to Central Park to read and enjoy nature. There is peace in solitude, and she felt her best when alone.

Sam had classes during the week, so most of their plans were on the weekends, but often, Onyx couldn't make it because she worked most weekends and nights.

Eventually, Onyx met Blake through Sam at a party. Onyx and Blake went on a date. He was handsome and funny, but Onyx was still trying to determine if she liked him enough to go out with him again. After all, that was the first time she'd been on a date.

She felt awkward during the first date and was sure he would not be interested in seeing her again, but he continued to text.

Onyx was not your average girl. She was an eccentric introvert who preferred to be alone, so she didn't interact well with others, and Blake was intrigued by her personality. He liked her as she was and was doing everything he could to win her over.

Fall finally arrived, Onyx's favorite season. She enjoyed how the leaves changed color, and everything was outwardly dying, only to bloom again in spring.

One night on the train heading to work, Onyx observed two teenage boys harassing an older man and felt the rage she had so arduously worked on come alive.

One kid punched the man in the face, and she was on her feet before realizing it. Onyx had purchased a stun gun on the internet and was willing to try it out. So she walked up to the kid that punched the older man and zapped him on the neck, longer than the instructions suggested.

The other one screamed and was about to hit her, but Onyx kicked his knee and zapped him in the face.

The train stopped, and she got off, quickly walking out of the station. It wasn't her stop, but she wasn't going to stick around.

Stun guns were illegal, and people recorded the incident instead of lending a helping hand. "*Make good choices*," she heard the doc say in her head.

Now, every day was beginning to feel the same. Her life was a dull monotony, and she was starting to feel apathetic again, as if a dark cloud were looming over her, preventing her from seeing the light.

The anxiety would creep up and suffocate her now and then, and she felt indifferent about things she had enjoyed before.

"Hey, what's going on? I feel like you're avoiding me," Blake asked over the phone.

"Oh, it's work. I've been exhausted and sleeping a lot during the day," Onyx told him, wanting to end the call.

What she disliked the most about dating and having friends was the emotional neediness of people. She was unable to relate, making them feel like she was distant or as if they'd done something wrong, and Onyx didn't know how to explain it. The more she interacted with others, she realized how complicated people were and how wonderful it was to be alone. She also wondered how Dr. Seeland would analyze her feelings in that regard.

She and Blake had been dating for a few months now. She spent the holidays with him and his family. They were lively and fun, and she was happy that Blake was in her life and that his family was welcoming and accepting of her. She was also grateful for Blake's patience as often, she didn't want to see or talk to him, but he didn't give up on her.

The night before meeting Blake's family, Onyx had an awful panic attack in anticipation.

"*You have to love yourself, Onyx,*" Dr. Seeland said. "*What others think of you is none of your business, but if you can't accept yourself, how can you expect others to do so?*" she recalled, attempting to calm down.

"*We receive what we transmit,*" Dr. Seeland said to her during their last session.

"Oh, shut up, Doc!" she had yelled to no one, attempting to gasp for air during the panic attack.

She had seen Dr. Seeland only a few times since dating Blake. "He's wonderful, thoughtful, sweet, loving … but I don't feel the connection. Sometimes, I think I'm with him out of boredom, and because

I love his family so much, I like feeling like I'm a part of them," she confessed to Dr. Seeland.

"There is nothing wrong with that. You're figuring this out while you battle anxiety and depression. Dating is new to you. So accept Blake's love but don't beat yourself up; don't try to force yourself to be or act in unnatural ways," she told Onyx.

Onyx nodded. "I just want to feel more engaged, more emotionally available; you know what I mean?"

Dr. Seeland smiled. "Onyx, you've been in survival mode your entire life. You did not have a model for love and affection. People who grow up in safe, loving environments full of affection and those who grow up trying to survive have different ways of expressing themselves emotionally and showing love. You're doing the best you can with what you have. But again, don't try to put yourself in a mold. Don't behave from the one-size-fits-all model. Be honest and do your best. That's all you can do," Dr. Seeland told her.

Onyx needed to hear that.

She often found herself trying to do what she felt was the societal standard of doing things, and most of it was draining and unnatural.

Dr. Seeland had advised her to be open about her childhood traumas and mental health struggles to give Blake a better understanding of her behavior.

"He has to accept you as you are," she told her.

Blake did accept Onyx as she was. He wasn't the problem. The problem is that she felt inadequate, like he deserved so much better.

She was battling those feelings in this relationship and managing them as best she could.

Blake was incredibly understanding. He gave her space whenever she felt overwhelmed and didn't want to talk or see him.

Blake planned a trip to Punta Cana, Dominican Republic, for her nineteenth birthday. Onyx's parents were both Dominican, and she was excited about the trip. She had never before left New York.

Now, Sam was acting strange, telling Onyx she was neglecting her for Blake, and Onyx could not understand how people could manage all these relationships without losing their minds.

PART NINETEEN

April was here. Onyx was ready to travel, and for the first time in her life, she was truly and genuinely excited about something.

It was a short flight. The airport was not far from the all-inclusive hotel. The beach was breathtaking, with gorgeous white sands that felt warm between Onyx's toes and heavenly blue waters.

The scent of the sea salt was distinctive. It was like nothing Onyx had ever smelled before. The sound of the waves was melodious as they crashed on the shore.

Onyx ran onto the beach with childlike glee and splashed in the water. She twirled around with delight, raising her face toward the sun. It was warm and bright, and she instantly felt happy and energized.

She was wearing a yellow bikini, and Blake felt like his girl was the prettiest one in the world as he watched her enjoy each moment.

There was a whole world Onyx didn't know, and she wanted to see all of it. But instead, she spent so much time in her head, worried, scared, and choking with anxiety, plagued by depression, that she could not enjoy life fully.

After this experience, Onyx was determined to overcome all of it and give her life the purpose and the meaning it lacked.

She sat on the sand next to Blake, sipping a frozen drink from a colorful straw with a cute umbrella. The horizon changed colors as the sun set, with orange, gold, yellow, red, purple, and pink hues. It was beautiful. She just sat and watched in awe as the sun finally disappeared on the horizon.

Blake kissed her passionately, and the rest of the trip felt like a honeymoon.

That summer, she went on a girl's trip to Miami with Sam and her friends. It was amazing. The beach was also beautiful but crowded, with beautiful faces, colorful bathing suits adorning stunning bodies, laughter, music, bicycles, and skates. It was like she had traveled to a different dimension.

They went dancing and had a lot of fun. Onyx was getting better at interacting with people, although she punched a guy in the face at a club for pulling her arm.

"Onyx, what is *wrong* with you?" Sam asked, mortified.

"I don't like strangers touching me. It's fucking weird," she said to her, storming out and returning to the hotel room.

When the girls returned that night, Onyx was already asleep. Nevertheless, they all laughed about the incident the following day over breakfast.

Onyx was relieved that it wasn't as big a deal as she had thought. Although she figured they wouldn't want to hang out with her anymore, she had to work on her anger and propensity for violence.

After an incident like that one, Onyx always remembered that dream. The one that felt like a life awaited her in the future, and she was afraid that she would make all the poor choices that would lead her to that life. The only thing in that life worth having was Mateo.

When Onyx returned to New York, she broke up with Blake.

"It's not you. It's me," she told him. Even though it might sound cliché, it was the truth. "You deserve better. My heart is just not in it," Onyx admitted.

"*Always be honest about your feelings, Onyx,*" Seeland said. "*Don't prioritize anyone's feelings over your own, or you'll become resentful,*" the doc warned her.

Onyx had to admit that the doc gave the best advice, and she listened.

At the end of the summer, Onyx booked a trip to California. Traveling alone was scary, but she felt exhilarated about it. If she could do this, she could do anything.

She had gotten her driver's license and rented a car. Then she went to the famous beaches, the Walk of Fame, the Hollywood sign, and Disneyland.

She had been taking online psychology classes now too. She wanted to be a child therapist to help children in foster care, but it was mostly to allow her to understand herself better.

She had even gotten a promotion at work, and things were going well. She worked long hours and didn't see Sam as much anymore either.

Maurice was a coworker. He and Onyx started hanging out. She felt comfortable with him, like she could be herself. He helped with changing things up. "You want to go to a gay bar?" he asked one day.

"I'm not twenty-one yet, remember?" she scolded.

"Girl, please. I can get you in. I used to date the bouncer at the door. You in or not?" Maurice asked. She shook her head but agreed to come.

They danced and drank all night. Finally, Onyx had too much to drink and vomited on the train ride home.

Maurice laughed. "Look at this rookie," he said as he recorded her, and Onyx snatched the phone from his hand.

"I may be drunk, but I can still kick your ass," she told him.

They laughed as she tried to kick him and fell.

Work was more exciting now that she and Maurice were friends. He was funny, and their shift went by quickly.

Onyx had an appointment with Dr. Seeland, and she canceled it because she and Maurice had gone out again, and she was hungover.

"*Make good choices,*" she heard the doc say in her head and laughed.

"Onyx, what have you been up to, girl? I rarely see you anymore," Sam said to her one day as they ran into each other on the staircase.

"Just busy with work," Onyx said on her way down.

"We need to catch up," Sam said.

"Definitely," Onyx promised as she went into her apartment.

People develop connections that Onyx doesn't understand, having never experienced attachment to anyone, and a bunch of Dr. Seeland's theories on developmental responses came to mind.

She was going on a date with Maurice's younger brother, Jordan. They hung out before, but Maurice was always there.

Jordan picked her up and took her to a hibachi restaurant in Westchester County. They ate a lot. She had steak and shrimp with rice and noodles, and he had steak with chicken.

She wore a plain black dress with sandals which she purchased from Jungle online with her employee discount. Jordan wore a plain white tee, blue jeans, and white sneakers.

After dinner, Jordan drove her home, and they sat in the car for a long time, talking. Jordan was in the army, and Onyx was fascinated to hear all about it.

They kissed and talked some more. "You're very mysterious," he said, playing with her hair, and she laughed.

"I'm fucked up in the head, but mysterious sounds better," she said, and they laughed again.

She thanked him for a lovely evening and went to her apartment. She wasn't into Jordan romantically, and she suggested they just remain friends after a few more dates.

"You're better off with someone normal. I'm just not ready to see anyone right now," Onyx told him when he insisted she give it another chance.

"Normal? What is normal?" Dr. Seeland asked her once when she brought up that she wasn't normal.

Onyx had told her it was what people do, or how they behave, all the things she had trouble with, and the doctor had responded with, "I see a lot of people, Onyx, and all of them are miserable. You know why?" and Onyx had no idea.

"They all want to be 'normal' instead of being themselves. So don't aspire to be like anyone else or to do things how others do them. Instead, be yourself, and do whatever the hell you want. As long as you don't hurt or damage others, who cares what anyone thinks," she told Onyx.

That was her all-time favorite Dr. Seeland quote. She repeated it to herself daily, but now, she said, "Fuck what people think. I don't care," and it made everything better. She felt free.

"Every so often, that dream comes to mind. I've had others, but that one in which I was on a quest to save the world and ended up losing someone I cared about still haunts me. I can still vividly recall details, places, and the characters in the dream. I call them characters because I have never seen them before. I go to places from the dream, and they're there, but not all. Some don't exist, like there is no Orion headquarters, but the motel

in the Bronx is there, the diner in Manhattan is there, only the names are different, but they exist. It's mind-boggling. It feels like I time-traveled in my dreams. Is that possible?"

"I started reading books on theoretical physics and remembered that I was a self-taught physicist in the dream."

She laughed as she wrote this in her journal. Onyx enjoyed herself. She felt like her best conversations were with herself, then thinks she's gone mad and schedules an appointment with Dr. Seeland, whom she likes because she thinks the doctor herself is crazy.

Like attracts like, she thought whenever the doc goes on some crazy rant.

Now she wondered if she could sleep travel to the past to re-create it. Onyx spent her nights imagining that she had a different childhood, where her parents were alive, loving, and nurturing. Where she developed deep bonds with them. But, of course, this was Dr. Seeland's suggestion.

She believed that the mind could not distinguish between reality and imagination, so it might create new neurological pathways that can impact Onyx's personality.

Onyx was beginning to feel dissatisfied with her work and wanted something different. She can better deal with people now, so she applied to other fields of work.

This weekend, she planned to go out with Sam and her friends. *It's been awhile*, Onyx thought, and she did promise Sam they'd catch up.

Onyx sensed having met Sam before but couldn't quite place it. She knocked on Sam's door. "You ready?" she asked when Sam answered.

"No, not yet. Come in," Sam said, walking away.

Onyx had never been in her apartment. "Where's your mom?" she asked, looking around.

"She's away visiting my grandmother," Sam said.

Onyx sat on the couch, and Sam sat next to her. "What's up with you, Onyx? I feel like you've been avoiding me," Sam asked.

Onyx felt uncomfortable. She wasn't sure what Sam meant. They had not hung out in a while because she was spending more time with Maurice and time alone, but it had nothing to do with her.

"Tell people exactly what you think, Onyx, and exactly how you feel. Don't prioritize anyone's feelings over your own," the doc always told her.

"Look, Sam, I don't know what you mean, but I like being alone most of the time, I have a new friend, and I've been doing different things with him. We have similar schedules because we work together. You and I are cool, but hanging out with people constantly drains me. It has nothing to do with you. I just need to take breaks from socializing to recharge, that's all," Onyx told her, annoyed that she had to explain herself.

Sam relaxed. "Oh, because I thought like I had done something you didn't like, and you didn't want to hang out anymore," she said, relieved.

Suddenly, Sam leaned in and touched Onyx's face. "You're so beautiful, and I like you a lot. Our friendship means the world to me, that's all," she said, now lightly kissing Onyx on the lips.

Onyx sat there in shock, not knowing what Sam meant by the kiss. *Whatever*, she thought and frowned. *People are so fucking dramatic. So what if I didn't want to hang out with her anymore?* she thought.

"No, that's just the way I am. You can take or leave it," Onyx said triumphantly.

A few years, or even months ago, she would've been worried about keeping this friendship, but now, she didn't care. "And what's with the kiss? You into me like that?" she asked Sam, wanting to clear that up.

"Don't be silly," Sam said, slapping her hand. "Unless you are," she said with a strange look.

"No, I'm not," Onyx said, hoping things didn't get awkward between them.

Sam laughed. "Relax. Let me finish getting ready so we can be on our way," she said. Sam came out wearing a beautiful short red dress with black heels.

Onyx ran into Blake at that party. "Hey, how have you been? You look as beautiful as ever." He was always so sweet.

Onyx was wearing shorts and a crop top with sandals. "I've been well. How about you? How's your family?" she asked.

"All good. My mom is always asking about you. We all miss you," he said sadly. "Maybe we can catch up one of these days, huh?"

Onyx gave him a closed-lipped smile. Blake recognized it. It was the one she gave when she didn't want to hurt your feelings or was about to say something bluntly.

"Blake, I don't want to give you false hope. What would be the point of catching up if you have expectations that I'm not going to fulfill," she said.

Blake smiled. There was that brutal honesty he admired. "Onyx, we can be friends. It's OK, I promise," he told her. She just nodded.

That's the issue with people. They like to delude themselves with comfortable lies. So he says it's OK, knowing he'd like to be more than friends, and he was willing to put himself in painful situations because he convinced himself he could win her back.

It is much simpler to let go. Anything that no longer wants to be in our lives, anything that no longer serves us, and anything that causes us pain … needs to be released.

"Sure, OK," she said, defeated. What was the use? He'd only keep insisting.

PART TWENTY

Onyx had not seen Dr. Seeland in weeks. So what would she say about Blake? Indeed, she would have an excellent interpretation. Still, Onyx felt she handled it correctly.

Dr. Seeland advised being honest about your feelings, and Onyx was much more comfortable doing that.

Often, we tell people what they want to hear instead of how we feel, causing ourselves heartache and pain. Putting the needs of others above our own is a recipe for unhappiness. However, Onyx did miss Blake in a Platonic way. There was nothing more she wanted than to like him, love him, and be in a relationship with him. She tried to force it, but it didn't happen, making her angry. Her inability to forge those bonds frustrated her, making her feel broken.

She missed Blake's family. Spending time with them was fun if being only friends was OK with him. She would not oppose that. It would be nice to be part of his life as friends. However, there was no way he would try to move into a relationship again after she had made herself clear.

Onyx started a new job as a teacher's assistant in a public elementary school. She was nervous. She wasn't sure how she would do with small children. So she lied in the interview and said she loved kids and was excellent with them, but doesn't everyone lie at interviews?

She would soon find out because it was Monday, and she was on her way …

The good thing about this job was that she had weekends and holidays off and laughed at herself. *But what good is having weekends and holidays off when you never have plans because you have very few friends and no family?* she thought.

The not-so-good thing about the job is that she had to transition from working nights. There was a beauty to working nights that any introvert can relate to because fewer people were around. But now, she had to be ready to conquer the world and be forced to function in an everyday setting.

Onyx felt confident she could manage regular working hours and be around larger groups of people and children. After all, what's the worst thing that can happen?

"*Do more things that scare you; challenge yourself,*" the doc said.

It was September. The year was almost over. Another year was gone, and she felt proud of how far she had come.

"Adulting isn't that bad. I'm better at it than I was at being a child," she had told Dr. Seeland.

The doc replied, "*Because you were never really a child, your survival instinct kicked in early on and cut your childhood short. Most children feel safe and protected with their parents and caregivers, but you were never able to develop those bonds, which prevented you from feeling safe,*" or something along those lines.

It didn't matter now. Onyx felt good taking care and looking out for herself. She still struggled with her depression, but she was learning to manage it better. She talked herself out of the sadness and got up every day, determined to find something good instead of wallowing in despair.

"*It is your choice. You can choose to be miserable, or you can be happy, but stop feeling sorry for yourself,*" Dr. Seeland told her

The new job wasn't at all what she expected. However, she had no trouble getting along with her coworkers, nodding, smiling, participating in small talk, and looking interested. The problem was the screaming, unruly kids. How on earth do the parents do it? she asked herself daily.

Some days were rewarding, and helping the children learn different things was fun, but kindergarten was no joke. As Onyx discovered who she was, she realized that working with children was not for her.

She went to the movies with Blake, and it was a disaster. During the film, he tried to hold her hand, which infuriated her. "You're such a fucking idiot. Lose my number, asshole!" she said, storming out before the movie had concluded.

It had been awhile since her anger got the best of her. Maybe it was the new job. It was only a matter of time before she snapped.

"Why do you think you reacted that way? Why were you so upset?" Dr. Seeland asked when she went to see her and told her about the incident.

"Because I fucking told him. I told him there was no sense in remaining friends if he still wanted something more, and the liar insisted, 'no, it's OK,'" she said, imitating Blake at the end.

Dr. Seeland laughed. "I understand. People say what they think we want to hear and then do what they want to do. However, you cannot surrender your power that way. What I mean is whatever angers you controls you. So, learn to be a neutral observer whenever possible. You could have walked out on him without the angry out-burst. I find it amusing, don't you, now that you think about it?" she asked Onyx.

Onyx smiled. She did find it funny now. She told herself, "Damn, girl, you're crazy," and laughed aloud on the train ride home, attracting strange looks from other passengers, but she didn't care. She got those looks often.

"Listen, Dr. Seeland, I've been doing good. I override the urge to punch people in the face daily. So give me some credit here. I wanted to punch him and didn't. But the truth is, I was glad and honestly hoping something like that would happen finally to have Blake out of my life for good," she confessed.

"Blake loves you, and it's challenging to let go of love, but you were honest, and you've come a long way, Onyx. I'm proud of you," Dr. Seeland told her.

"It's all thanks to you, Doc," Onyx said with a smile.

"How is your new job?" she asked, and Onyx frowned.

"If I'm being honest, I fucking hate it. Those kids are Chucky on steroids. I need to find something else before I rip off someone's head," Onyx said, and they laughed. Then she promised to come regularly when the visit was over.

Onyx called out from work. She was feeling peculiar. She had flashes of memories she had never before experienced. She felt odd, like she was stuck in a loop or having an out-of-body experience. Like she was observing her life unfold from the outside. She feared Dr. Seeland would be at a loss for words with this one.

Could anyone understand what she was feeling? Do you? Does this happen to other people? What was the meaning of the disconnect she felt between her sense of self and her life?

It's like a "waking" dream, where you witness the events happening with a sense of helplessness. She had a solid urge to run away, but from what exactly? Could it be a defense mechanism?

The mind deconstructs everything it thinks it is and knows in a desperate attempt to create something new.

What is God? Onyx always wondered. She admired Alma and her conviction in her faith but felt that religion was the experience of others, passed down through generations. She wondered what it was like to experience God for herself. Is *that* what was happening? People don't question anything. They accept everything with the excuse that that's the way it is.

Onyx found the advantage of her childhood. No one cared enough to upload their beliefs, ideals, and customs to her consciousness, so she felt free to choose and experience things for herself.

Dr. Seeland once said, "*We have been conditioned since birth and need to free ourselves to find our truth.*"

Is that what she was experiencing? A desire to liberate herself from human conditioning? That best explained how she felt … caged, trapped as if life were suffocating her, or rather the concept of life she had witnessed, or maybe the simple explanation was that she was mad, crazy, or insane.

What did it mean to be insane? To perceive things unconventionally than others, or rather unacceptably?

Why try to find some profound metaphysical explanation for madness? Could it be that those deemed crazy were the few who have set themselves free from this consciousness prison?

Human awareness is narrow. It is not appropriate to speak about these things. People are afraid to explore beyond what is acceptable. Maybe that is why so many are allegedly mentally ill.

Onyx had no one to discuss this with, so she scheduled an appointment with Dr. Seeland.

Dr. Seeland listened to Onyx attentively. She was worried about this new crisis. "Onyx, you need to find your life's purpose. That is why you feel this way. You are dissatisfied with life and cannot find fulfillment. Remember, life doesn't have to be elaborate. Be content with just being; live each day with wonder," Dr. Seeland told her.

"I've been doing that for the past year, and it's been working, but I can't shake these feelings off and find the proper way to express them. Maybe you're too close to me and don't want to diagnose me with anything beyond trauma. Just admit that I'm clinically insane. It'll help me feel better," Onyx pleaded.

"Onyx, you're not insane. First, figure out who you are, and when you do, you will better understand what you need. If this is some spiritual awakening, then visit different religious institutions. Read sacred books, find self-help information, and delve into this new experience until you discover what rings true for you, but please don't give so much importance to inconsequentialities. You are spending far too much energy on this. Don't let this consume you. Don't skip out on life because you feel lost. Instead, learn to navigate the array of emotions as they surface, and learn to love yourself there," she told Onyx.

Onyx shrugged her shoulders, wishing she would have told her she was crazy instead.

"The senses limit human perception. Sure, there is probably far more we cannot see, hear, or touch, and perhaps, some people, like you, may be sensitive to an energetic field beyond our traditional comprehension. I don't think anyone is insane in how it is traditionally defined. However, I feel some are tapping into dimensions that are not in conventional physical reality, and anything that is not scientifically understood is relegated to a realm of fiction or anomaly," she continued.

Onyx sat quietly for a long time, taking in everything Dr. Seeland said. She didn't see her as a therapist anymore. Instead, she saw her as a friend, and there was no one else she could freely talk with about these topics.

"I guess I'm torn between my fears and insecurities and a relentless self-awareness of power. Those two notions are contradictory, and that frightens me," Onyx said.

"Please elaborate," Dr. Seeland encouraged her.

"I keep thinking about that dream, the one in which that aspect of myself dies, and I felt devasted. I want to work toward that, being the best version of myself, but I cannot help but admire the Onyx I was in that dream. Yes, she was flawed, but she was fearless and confident and found happiness with Jones and love in Mateo, and I haven't found any of those things yet," Onyx said.

Dr. Seeland didn't speak. Instead, she looked at Onyx, eager to hear more.

"I'm trying to say that I need to be Onyx, disconnected, emotionally unavailable, angry, and alone before I can become Mateo. So I accept myself here, love myself precisely that way, and I've decided to live empowered as she did," Onyx continued.

Dr. Seeland smiled. "My dear, that is what I have been saying all this time, and I think you've finally figured it out."

After this visit with Dr. Seeland, Onyx felt good and realized it was not the doctor's responsibility to make her feel good. It was her own.

Onyx didn't tell her, but that would be the last time she would see Dr. Seeland, not because she felt healed or because Onyx knew all her inner struggles would be gone, but because the doc had equipped her with the tools to figure it out for herself.

She was no longer interested in being anything other than herself. Finally, Onyx accepted that her experiences had shaped her into the person she is.

She would in no way use that as an excuse to be a shitty person, but she would not continue to torture herself with the desire to be like everyone else.

Onyx was going to be the Onyx Pion Kyle despised. The Onyx Pion Jones enjoyed. The Onyx Pion Pablo thought was perfect, and the Onyx Pion Mateo wanted to save.

She will set herself free. It wasn't her inadequacies she feared. No, her power, strength, and resilience scared her. Her perceived flaws were her best qualities and gave her the courage not to need anyone.

One day, Onyx was checking her email and saw an army advertisement. She stared at it for a while.

That could be fun. That could be the start of the life I want to live. Maybe that's what I'm missing. That's where she *started*, Onyx thought to herself.

She was sick of working at the school, so she decided to go for a run from Washington Heights to Harlem, where the local recruiting center was located.

Onyx stood outside the recruitment office for a while, asking herself if that was what she wanted to do. "Fuck it. I'll check it out," she said, going inside.

Only a few people were there, and she was reading a sign when a young man approached her.

"What can I do for you?" he asked with a smile.

Onyx stared at him, unable to answer.

His skin was golden, like the sun. His curly brown hair was longer on top, and his eyes, like honey, shimmered with confidence. He was tall, with ripped muscles.

Onyx had never seen anything so perfect in her entire life. It was as if the gods chiseled him. It wasn't precisely Mateo from her dream, but it *was* him. She recognized him immediately.

"Matthew Mendez. Nice to meet you," he said, extending his hand.

"M&M," she muffled.

"Yes, my friends from high school call me that. What's your name?" he asked.

She was ogling him in amazement. Was this a dream? Was she dreaming again?

"Onyx," she said finally.

"Nice name. Fitting," he said with that smile that brightened the room.

He should be a model, she thought.

"So, air force, navy—" but before he could finish, she asked, "What branch do you recruit for?"

"Army!" he said proudly.

"Are you the best recruiter in this region?" she asked, and he laughed.

"Absolutely not. Are you a reporter or something?" he countered.

Onyx smiled. "Absolutely not," she replied mockingly, and they both laughed.

"So, you want to join the army?" he questioned.

"I wanted to, but I just changed my mind," she told him.

No, Onyx wasn't going to be her. She wouldn't make the same mistakes if she wanted a different outcome.

Onyx had to do things differently. This was a second chance. There he was, alive, radiant, and perfect. She would not lose Mateo a second time. Everything she had wanted and prayed for since that dream was standing right in front of her. It might have been a dream, but it was a life lived. What if that was a potential future she had witnessed? Onyx could not do the same things and expect a different outcome.

Matthew looked at her, surprised. "That was fast. Why?" he asked.

Onyx grinned. "Because enlisting would take me away from those that matter and unleash a shitstorm," she said.

Now, Matthew laughed loudly. "I have to say, you're funny. Those that matter are fortunate, and how could you possibly know you will unleash a shitstorm?" he asked, puzzled.

She was laughing too. Mat's laughter was contagious. "Because I'm sort of a badass, and the army just isn't ready, and I'm the fortunate one. But if you'd like to convince me, take my number and put your recruiting skills to the test," she dared him.

He was intrigued. "Is that a challenge, young lady?" he asked.

She wrote her number on a pad on his desk. "It is!" she said, winking, and he smiled.

"You just made my day, so challenge accepted," he said, taking the paper as she handed it to him.

"You've made my lifetime," she sang as she left the office.

Once outside the building, she jumped up and down with excitement. Onyx wasn't sure why she was so happy, but she was.

It might sound cliché, but it's as if this was the moment Onyx had been waiting for her entire life. Finally, a meeting, a connection, perhaps not in a romantic sense, but like she finally found her place in the world.

Often, people confuse that with a physical location when all along, it is a person, or a group of people … the tribe meant to journey with you through life.

No matter the time or space, once you find them, the colors in your life change, and you find the meaning and purpose you have been yearning for and come alive.

Dr. Seeland harped on and on about choices, and she was right. The doc was right about everything.

Maybe she would enlist and explore that as the other Onyx did, but for now, she wanted to explore the connection with Mat. She was determined to be a better version of herself for him.

"He's going to call me!" she shouted to a lady walking by, and the lady looked at her as if she were mad.

ABOUT THE AUTHOR

J.P. Ozuna was born in the Dominican Republic and emigrated to the United States at age four. 2030 is her debut novel; Ozuna is an avid reader and passionate writer. Currently, she lives with her beautiful family in Putnam County, New York.

www.platanopublishing.com

j.p.ozuna